This journal

BELONGS TO

· ·

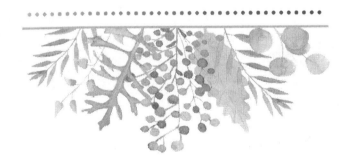

TOTALLY BOOKED
A Book Lover's Companion

Created and designed by
CAMRY CRIST

Printed in the U.S.A.

Contents

Truly the light is sweet,
and a pleasant thing it is
for the eyes to behold the sun.

ECCLESIASTES 11 : 7

AN

INTRODUCTION

"She read books as one would breathe air, to fill up and live."
—Annie Dillard

Book lovers are special people. They know how to live more than one life by opening the pages of a book. They know how to travel, how to dream, and how to explore. Studies show book lovers are more in touch with their emotions, more open-minded, less stressed, and more willing to learn new things. They even develop a greater empathy for others and what they are going through.

When we read books, we are transformed. The characters touch our lives and, in a way, become our friends. Naturally, certain books remain fixed in our memories because they have moved us on a deep level.

We Mosaic authors want to support you on your reading journey. We value book lovers, and we are as excited as you are that there are thousands of books out there waiting to be devoured. We are honored each time you choose to invest your precious reading time with a book from the Mosaic Collection, and are even more touched when you write a review of one of our books. May God bless your reading journey!

To learn more about each author and to discover her books, visit www.mosaiccollectionbooks.com/about-the-authors

WE'D LOVE TO HEAR FROM YOU

We'd appreciate your feedback as we design Mosaic's 2022 companion journal. We invite your comments at
www.mosaiccollectionbooks.com/totally-booked

The Mosaic Collection

OUR BOOKS

When Mountains Sing by Stacy Monson

Unbound by Eleanor Bertin

The Red Journal by Deb Elkink

A Beautiful Mess by Brenda S. Anderson

Hope is Born: A Mosaic Christmas Anthology

More Than Enough by Lorna Seilstad

The Road to Happenstance by Janice L. Dick

This Side of Yesterday by Angela D. Meyer

Lost Down Deep by Sara Davison

The Mischief Thief by Johnnie Alexander

Before Summer's End: A Mosaic Summer Anthology

Tethered by Eleanor Bertin

Calm Before the Storm by Janice L. Dick

Heart Restoration by Regina Rudd Merrick

Pieces of Granite by Brenda S. Anderson

Watercolors by Lorna Seilstad

A Star Will Rise: A Mosaic Christmas Anthology II

Eye of the Storm by Janice L. Dick

Behold, I am doing a new thing;
now it springs forth,
do you not perceive it?

ISAIAH 43 : 19A

MOSAIC

AUTHORS

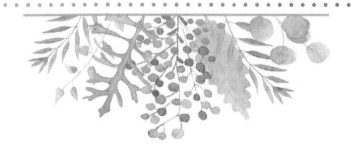

The Mosaic Collection

THE AUTHORS

Johnnie Alexander

Brenda S. Anderson

Eleanor Bertin

Sara Davison

Janice L. Dick

Deb Elkink

Chautona Havig

Regina Rudd Merrick

Angela D. Meyer

Stacy Monson

Lorna Seilstad

Marion Ueckermann

Candace West

Johnnie Alexander

MOSAIC AUTHOR

> Be brave and trust in God's steadfast love for you.

One of the first verses I ever claimed as my own was Proverbs 31:25. The translation I love most reads: *Strength and dignity are her clothing, and she smiles at the future.*

The first part of the verse is almost a mantra, a phrase I repeat to myself when I need courage. Maybe I'm faced with something as simple as a phone call I don't want to make. Or maybe the situation is much more serious. An ectopic pregnancy. Family tensions. Divorce. A dying parent.

During a difficult time in my life, I found a ceramic bluebird adorned with daisies and the words *Be Brave* in a gift shop. A clear and sweet whisper surrounded me.

It's for you!

The little bird now sits where I see it every day. Yes, life takes courage. And at the heart of courage—true courage—is trust. We can smile at the future, no matter what, because of God's steadfast love and His promise of eternal life with Him.

Johnnie's Mosaic Books

MOSAIC ANTHOLOGIES
Before Summer's End
Hope is Born

ROSE & THORNE
The Mischief Thief

Brenda G. Anderson

MOSAIC AUTHOR

See the heart that God sees and loves!

Listen...

Everyone has their own backstory that molds their beliefs and opinions and brings them to where they are in life. The problem is, we live in a reactionary world where we don't listen to what others are saying and, too often, we fail to hear all sides of a story. Rather, we react to opinions by pointing fingers. We're not only quick to say "You're wrong" but often resort to name calling and forget that this is a person whom God loves.

In each of my books, God has placed characters on my heart that I would normally struggle with: an arrogant businessman, a bully, mugger, collection agent, to name a few. With each character, God has shown me, "I love them. I want you to listen to them and see the heart that I see."

My hope is that through my stories, we open our ears and our eyes to see who God sees, hears, and loves...

Brenda's Mosaic Books

MOSAIC ANTHOLOGIES
A Star Will Rise
Before Summer's End
Hope is Born

Pieces of Granite
A Beautiful Mess

Eleanor Bertin

MOSAIC AUTHOR

God's truth holds fast, His love holds you and His grace never fails.

As a young girl, I relished the thrill of feeling tiny under a giant prairie sky, or counting the sparkling night stars. Like holding hands with a grizzly bear, God's thundering bigness against my feeble smallness terrifies and quiets me. That shivery awe fills the Bible with God's pure goodness and His never-ending love for sinners like me, in the sacrificial death of His Son Jesus in my place.

In my writing, I long to convey God's holiness and His mercy. I'm flooded with joy knowing I belong to a trustworthy, loving God who forgives me and never leaves me.

For nearly four decades, He has shown His providential care for my large family, from the smallest of details to the impossible dream of owning a home in the country.

Learning to trust Him in the daily things of life has been practice for trusting Him in the painful, and tragic. In 2012, our son Paul (18) was killed by a hit-and-run driver. In confusion and grief, I clung to the promises of scripture because Jesus has proved ever-faithful.

Eleanor's Mosaic Books

MOSAIC ANTHOLOGIES

A Star Will Rise
Before Summer's End
Hope is Born

TIES THAT BIND

Lifelines
Unbound
Tethered

Sara Davison

MOSAIC AUTHOR

> God is good.
> He will never leave
> or forsake you.

God never promised believers that life would be easy—He promised that He would never leave us or forsake us. I hope that this message, the core of all my stories, encourages readers when they are going through difficult times. We often don't understand why God allows certain things to happen to us or those we love, but we can trust that He is good, He is sovereign and in control, and He will never leave us.

As C.S. Lewis said, "I know now, Lord, why you utter no answer. You are yourself the answer. Before your face questions die away. What other answer would suffice?" I pray that all my readers, whatever they are going through, will know that they can trust that God's heart aches with ours, that He is always with us, and that one day He will set all things right.

Sara's Mosaic Books

MOSAIC ANTHOLOGIES
A Star Will Rise
Before Summer's End
Hope is Born

THE ROSE TATTOO TRILOGY
Lost Down Deep

Janice L. Dick

MOSAIC AUTHOR

> God is faithful and longs to draw us into a relationship with himself.

Tough times come to us all, but in spite of our best intentions, we don't always respond well. As I write, I often struggle with my own challenges through my characters. I don't have the answers, but I have faith in the One who does.

God's mercy reaches each of us in our particular situation, no matter how we respond. He is gracious and ever faithful to walk alongside, guiding us back to Himself. He is our hope.

Jan's Mosaic Books

MOSAIC ANTHOLOGIES
Hope is Born

HAPPENSTANCE CHRONICLES
The Road to Happenstance

THE STORM SERIES
Calm Before the Storm
Eye of the Storm

Deb Elkink

MOSAIC AUTHOR

look for God in the Bible;
all else merely points
to Him.

I'm a fiction writer with an imaginative mind but, before looking inward for story ideas, I study Scripture in order to retell timeless truths.

Of course, we see the thumbprint of the Creator everywhere, glimpsing Him in nature, history, culture, and relationships. But we need more than fleeting glimpses, don't we? Only the living, breathed-out Word of God can give us the knowledge and love our hearts are longing for. Though we read every other book in the world, the Bible is the only book that "reads" us, divinely challenging and changing us through Jesus.

So why do I write fiction? Good story entertains, connects, and elicits emotion, but it becomes downright powerful when undergirded by meaning. Fiction might not be fact (as the old adage goes), but it can nevertheless point to truth. Literature takes us through the make believe into matters of metaphysical and spiritual reality.

And so I love the Bible, for it applies wonderful truths to my soul that I can then express through imaginative writing.

Deb's
Mosaic Books

MOSAIC ANTHOLOGIES

Before Summer's End
Hope is Born

The Third Grace
The Red Journal

Chautona Havig

MOSAIC AUTHOR

Chautona's Mosaic Books

NEW TO MOSAIC!

First stories coming in 2021-2022

Using story to connect readers with the Master Storyteller.

I write to show that Christians are real, flawed, hurting, struggling people who have messy lives--to encourage them in their walks with Jesus. I *don't* write evangelistic fiction. That's not my strength. That's not to say I don't ever share Gospel elements. Of course, occasionally, someone in one of my books will come to Jesus. It'll happen sometimes. But I prefer to write that much how I prefer my romance—as a natural outpouring of a life lived rather than center stage. Not because I'm ashamed to share the gospel, but because fiction isn't how I choose to share it. Other authors do well with that, but I do not.

I write to "stimulate one another to love and good deeds." This is what my characters do. They are faced with situations and eventually approach the solution as they see Scripture advising. Here's a secret for you: I don't always agree with their solution. But the point is, they look to Jesus—His Word—for that solution. And that's my goal as an author. To encourage the body of Christ. *To turn to the Word of God, the Bible, for the solutions and inspirations in their lives—to use story to draw people back to the feet of the Master Storyteller.*

Regina Rudd Merrick

MOSAIC AUTHOR

Trust God and do the next right thing.

You are not alone. What you're going through is not unique to you. Life isn't a series of obstacles to overcome, but a series of events that point us to Jesus, who loves us more than we can imagine.

When I was a teen, I found myself doubting that I mattered, that God loved me, and that He wanted the best for me. When a move away from home and everything I held dear pulled the rug from under me, I distanced myself from God. It took a long time to trust Him again.

Now I write characters that know, deep down, that God loves them, and that He is in control. They have doubts, as I did. When I discovered my "life verse," Psalm 37:4, I realized I had such a small understanding. Eventually, I found that when I truly delight myself in the Lord, He will give me HIS desires, and they are infinitely superior to mine!

God is good, God is faithful, and God uses our brokenness to draw us closer to Him.

Regina's Mosaic Books

MOSAIC ANTHOLOGIES
A Star Will Rise
Hope is Born

RENO-VATIONS SERIES
Heart Restoration

Angela D. Meyer

MOSAIC AUTHOR

> God is able to heal,
> restore and redeem
> any brokenness.

There is brokenness everywhere we look, and people are turning to the world for answers. What the world offers will not suffice. Only God can make whole what has been shattered. I have experienced firsthand this redemptive, restorative power of God's grace in my marriage.

Several years ago, I discovered my husband had a sexual addiction. He repented and between counseling, an accountability group and the grace of God he is now an overcomer of sexual addiction.

While God helped my husband through his healing, God helped me as I worked through my anger and grieved over what had been lost. I learned to trust God more deeply. We aren't perfect by any stretch of the imagination, but God continues to give us grace in the midst of our imperfections.

There is always hope in Jesus and it's my heart to share through my stories that God is able to heal, restore and redeem any brokenness in our lives.

Angela's Mosaic Books

MOSAIC ANTHOLOGIES

A Star Will Rise
Hope is Born

This Side of Yesterday

Stacy Monson

MOSAIC AUTHOR

The truth of who you are is found in the love of the God of the Universe. You are the Beloved.

Who are you? And who gets to decide?

Our identity is found first and foremost in God. Made in His image, we bear His DNA. We are fully, unconditionally loved by our Creator. Society tells us we don't measure up, we aren't good enough, we need to conform. God tells us we are loved exactly as we are. He invites us daily to walk with Him, look to Him for whatever need, and trust Him no matter what happens to or around us. Despite the negative messages that drip constantly in our lives, His message shines through – you are loved.

Scripture reminds us that Christ died for us *while we were still sinners.* So regardless of how short we think we fall, how little we measure up, or how worthless we've been told we are, we are already heirs with Christ, a daughter of the Most High, perfect just as we are.

I am His beloved. So are you.

Stacy's Mosaic Books

MOSAIC ANTHOLOGIES
Before Summer's End
Hope is Born

MY FATHER'S HOUSE
When Mountains Sing

Lorna Geilstad

MOSAIC AUTHOR

God loves you more in this moment than anyone could in a lifetime.

Over and over, I see people searching for love. Sometimes this search leads them into relationships that are painful, but other times they still end up feeling like there's something missing. But the love of God is perfect and unfailing. We have a hard time understanding God's unconditional love. We cannot grasp the breadth or depth of it. We cannot earn His love and we don't have to. God loves us because He loves us and He is love.

Three years ago, my husband had a massive heart attack at the age of 57. His heart stopped for over 45 minutes, and he ended up in ICU. During the ten days of waiting, I faced paralyzing fear. What would I do without the man I loved? Then, I remember thinking that God loved me more than even my husband, and He loved me more in this horrible moment than anyone ever could. My husband did recover, and he's doing well today. While I know tomorrow holds no guarantees, I also know God is faithful.

Lorna's Mosaic Books

More Than Enough
Watercolors

Marion Ueckermann

MOSAIC AUTHOR

You are so special to God.
You are loved beyond measure.

God can take the blank or messed-up canvasses of our lives and turn each one into a masterpiece. His masterpiece.

I've seen it in people's lives, I experience it constantly in the lives of my characters with each book I write, and I've seen and experienced God's goodness and faithfulness and change in my own life.

As a teenager, I wasn't rotten or a rebel, but I was the child who walked a little closer to the wild side than my siblings. No doubt I kept my mother on her knees during those teen and young adult years. But God always drew me back into his fold, always went looking for me when I strayed. He has given me more than I could ever have asked for—an amazing husband, wonderful sons, and three adorable grandchildren. That's grace. That's undeserved favor.

Marion's Mosaic Books

MOSAIC ANTHOLOGIES
A Star Will Rise
Before Summer's End

Candace West

MOSAIC AUTHOR

Candace's Mosaic Books

MOSAIC ANTHOLOGIES
A Star Will Rise

Redemption through Jesus makes all things possible.

Needing forgiveness and granting forgiveness are the cornerstones of our experience. All of us have sinned and fallen short of God's grace. All of us have been wronged.

My writing journey embraces broken characters who need restoration.

As Lane Steen trudged across the fields of my imagination, her auburn hair grazed her cheeks, partially concealing a purple bruise. I had to know why. Her journey to forgiveness—needed and granted—began in the Valley Creek Redemption series.

When I wrote Lane Steen, I harbored my own heartache and brokenness. Even though I yearned to forgive, I discovered I couldn't. But then, through writing, God taught me a powerful, yet simple truth.

Forgiveness is an act of the will through the power of Jesus Christ. After this, my prayer became, "Lord, I can't forgive. If You'll help me, I'm willing."

The key to forgiveness is a willing heart.

Mosaic
SHELF LIFE

Color in one book on the shelf for each book or short story you've read that's written by a Mosaic author.

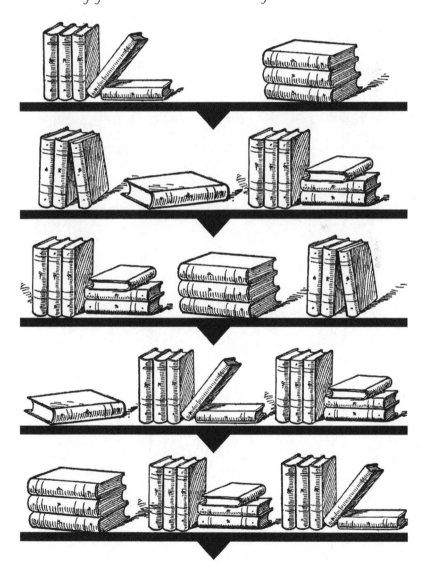

Ascribe greatness to our God.
He is the Rock, His work is perfect;
For all His ways are justice,
A God of truth and without injustice;
Righteous and upright is He.

DEUTERONOMY 32 : 3, 4

2020

YEAR IN REVIEW

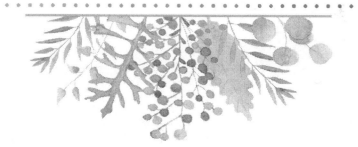

A Peek in the Mirror

FAVORITE BOOKS

_____
_____
_____
_____
_____

FAVORITE QUOTE

_____
_____
_____
_____
_____
_____
_____
_____
_____

FAVORITE NEW AUTHORS

_____
_____
_____
_____

BEST NEW RELEASES

_____
_____
_____
_____
_____

GREATEST SURPRISE

_____
_____
_____

Books Upon Books

TOTAL BOOKS READ

GENRE	# OF BOOKS
_____	_____
_____	_____
_____	_____
_____	_____
_____	_____
_____	_____

TOTAL BOOKS REVIEWED

AVERAGE RATING ☆ ☆ ☆ ☆ ☆

ENJOYABLE LAUNCH TEAMS

_____

_____

_____

_____

_____

_____

_____

_____

The LORD your God is in your midst,
a mighty one who will save;
he will rejoice over you with gladness;
he will quiet you by his love;
he will exult over you with loud singing.

ZEPHANIAH 3 : 17

2021

THE COMING YEAR

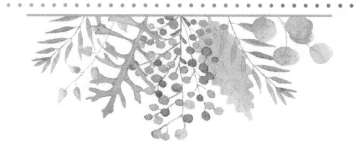

A Glance Ahead

HIGHLY ANTICIPATED NEW RELEASES

_____

_____

_____

_____

_____

_____

UPCOMING EVENTS

_____

_____

_____

ONE NEW AUTHOR TO TRY

_____

Book Wishlist

GENRE

-
-
-
-
-
-
-
-
-
-
-
-
-
-

Book Wishlist

GENRE

Book Wishlist

GENRE

-
-
-
-
-
-
-
-
-
-
-
-
-
-

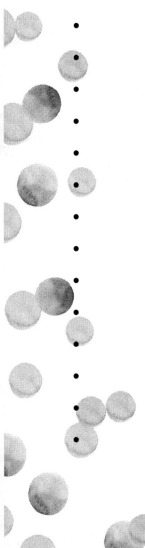

TBR

Book Wishlist

GENRE

-
-
-
-
-
-
-
-
-
-
-
-
-
-
-
-

Book Wishlist

GENRE

_____

-
-
-
-
-
-
-
-
-
-
-
-
-
-
-

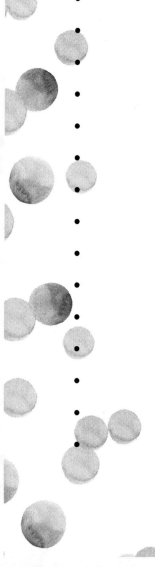

-
-
-
-
-
-
-
-
-
-
-
-
-

Reading Challenge

IDEAS

A book in a genre you don't normally read
A book by an author with your initials
A book published in the decade you were born
A book you chose because of the cover
A book with a color in the title
A book set in a place you'd like to travel to
A book that has been made into a movie
A book with a number in the title
A book with a one word title
A book based on a true story
A book with an animal on the cover
An award-winning book
A debut novel
A book with a red cover
An epistolary book
A book with a month of the year in the title
A book written by more than one author
An audiobook

Reading Challenge

JANUARY

_____

_____

_____

_____

FEBRUARY

_____

_____

_____

_____

MARCH

_____

_____

_____

_____

Reading Challenge

APRIL

_____

_____

_____

_____

MAY

_____

_____

_____

_____

JUNE

_____

_____

_____

_____

Reading Challenge

JULY

_____

_____

_____

_____

AUGUST

_____

_____

_____

_____

SEPTEMBER

_____

_____

_____

_____

Reading Challenge

OCTOBER

_____
_____
_____
_____

NOVEMBER

_____
_____
_____
_____

DECEMBER

_____
_____
_____
_____

Lord, you alone are my portion and my cup;
you make my lot secure.
The boundary lines have fallen for me
in pleasant places;
surely I have a delightful inheritance.

PSALM 16 : 5 - 6

2021

A CLOSER LOOK

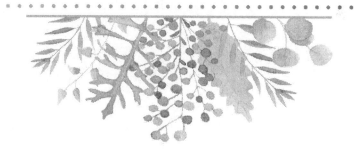

January

JANUARY GOALS

_____
_____
_____
_____

BEST READS

_____
_____
_____

BEST BOOKS REVIEWED

_____
_____
_____
_____
_____

FAVORITE QUOTES

_____

_____

_____

_____

_____

_____

_____

Color one for every book you read in January.

Reading Minutes

DAILY MINUTES READ CHART

☐	MINUTES I WANT TO READ THIS MONTH
☐	ACTUAL MINUTES I READ THIS MONTH

1	2	3	4	5	6	7
8	9	10	11	12	13	14
15	16	17	18	19	20	21
22	23	24	25	26	27	28
29	30	31				

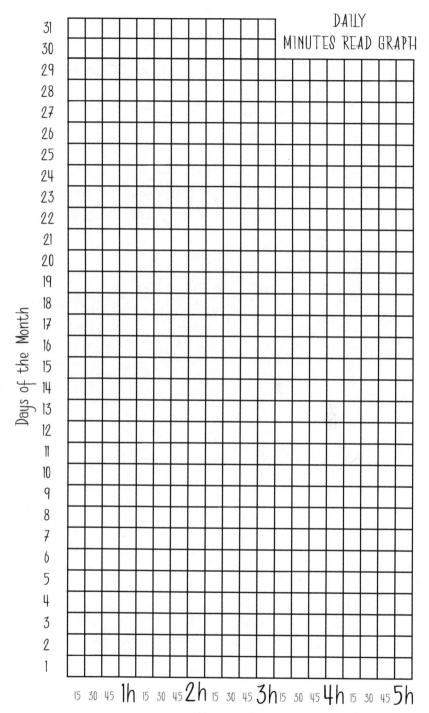

DAILY
MINUTES READ GRAPH

Days of the Month

31 30 29 28 27 26 25 24 23 22 21 20 19 18 17 16 15 14 13 12 11 10 9 8 7 6 5 4 3 2 1

15 30 45 1h 15 30 45 2h 15 30 45 3h 15 30 45 4h 15 30 45 5h

Minutes Read

February

FEBRUARY GOALS

_____

_____

_____

_____

BEST READS

_____

_____

_____

BEST BOOKS REVIEWED

_____

_____

_____

_____

_____

FAVORITE QUOTES

_____

_____

_____

_____

_____

_____

Color one for every book you read in February.

Reading Minutes

DAILY MINUTES READ CHART

☐ MINUTES I WANT TO READ THIS MONTH

☐ ACTUAL MINUTES I READ THIS MONTH

1	2	3	4	5	6	7
8	9	10	11	12	13	14
15	16	17	18	19	20	21
22	23	24	25	26	27	28
29	30	31				

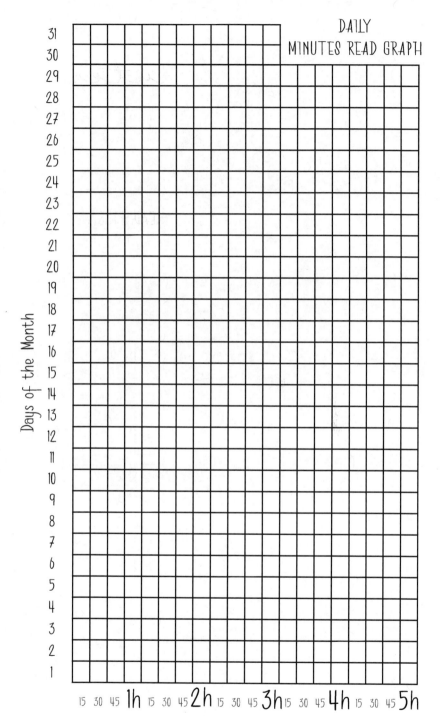

March

MARCH GOALS

_____

_____

_____

_____

BEST READS

_____

_____

_____

BEST BOOKS REVIEWED

_____

_____

_____

_____

_____

FAVORITE QUOTES

_____

_____

_____

_____

_____

_____

Color one for every book you read in March.

Reading Minutes

DAILY MINUTES READ CHART

	MINUTES I WANT TO READ THIS MONTH

	ACTUAL MINUTES I READ THIS MONTH

1	2	3	4	5	6	7
8	9	10	11	12	13	14
15	16	17	18	19	20	21
22	23	24	25	26	27	28
29	30	31				

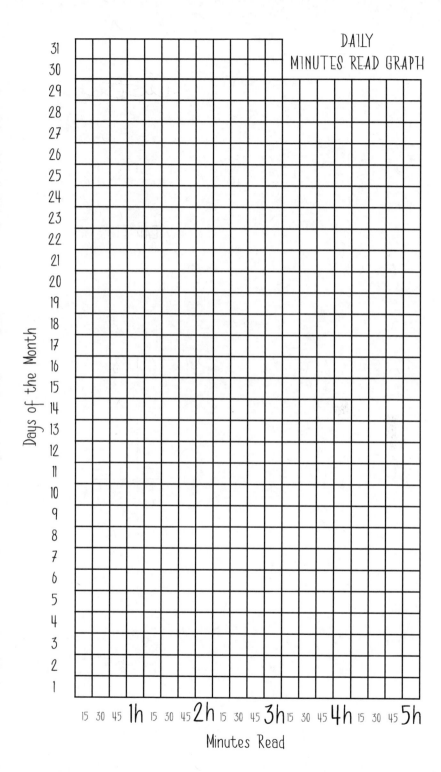

DAILY
MINUTES READ GRAPH

Days of the Month

31
30
29
28
27
26
25
24
23
22
21
20
19
18
17
16
15
14
13
12
11
10
9
8
7
6
5
4
3
2
1

15 30 45 **1h** 15 30 45 **2h** 15 30 45 **3h** 15 30 45 **4h** 15 30 45 **5h**

Minutes Read

April

APRIL GOALS

_____
_____
_____
_____

BEST READS

_____
_____
_____

BEST BOOKS REVIEWED

_____
_____
_____
_____
_____

FAVORITE QUOTES

_____

_____

_____

_____

_____

_____

Color one for every book you read in April.

Reading Minutes

DAILY MINUTES READ CHART

	MINUTES I WANT TO READ THIS MONTH
	ACTUAL MINUTES I READ THIS MONTH

1	2	3	4	5	6	7
8	9	10	11	12	13	14
15	16	17	18	19	20	21
22	23	24	25	26	27	28
29	30	31				

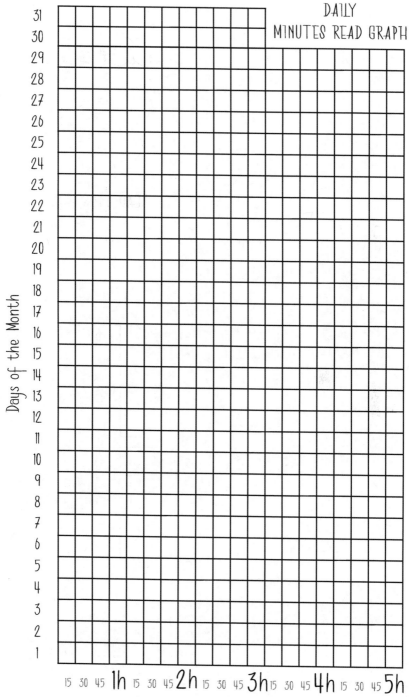

DAILY
MINUTES READ GRAPH

Days of the Month

31
30
29
28
27
26
25
24
23
22
21
20
19
18
17
16
15
14
13
12
11
10
9
8
7
6
5
4
3
2
1

15 30 45 1h 15 30 45 2h 15 30 45 3h 15 30 45 4h 15 30 45 5h

Minutes Read

May

MAY GOALS

_____

_____

_____

_____

BEST READS

_____

_____

_____

BEST BOOKS REVIEWED

_____

_____

_____

_____

_____

FAVORITE QUOTES

_____

_____

_____

_____

_____

_____

Color one for every book you read in May.

Reading Minutes

DAILY MINUTES READ CHART

	MINUTES I WANT TO READ THIS MONTH
	ACTUAL MINUTES I READ THIS MONTH

1	2	3	4	5	6	7
8	9	10	11	12	13	14
15	16	17	18	19	20	21
22	23	24	25	26	27	28
29	30	31				

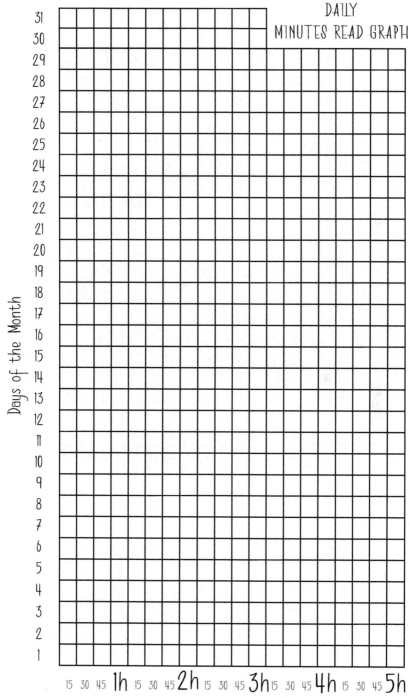

DAILY
MINUTES READ GRAPH

Days of the Month

15 30 45 1h 15 30 45 2h 15 30 45 3h 15 30 45 4h 15 30 45 5h

Minutes Read

June

JUNE GOALS

_____

_____

_____

_____

BEST READS

_____

_____

_____

BEST BOOKS REVIEWED

_____

_____

_____

_____

_____

FAVORITE QUOTES

_____

_____

_____

_____

_____

_____

Color one for every book you read in June.

Reading Minutes

DAILY MINUTES READ CHART

☐	MINUTES I WANT TO READ THIS MONTH
☐	ACTUAL MINUTES I READ THIS MONTH

1	2	3	4	5	6	7
8	9	10	11	12	13	14
15	16	17	18	19	20	21
22	23	24	25	26	27	28
29	30	31				

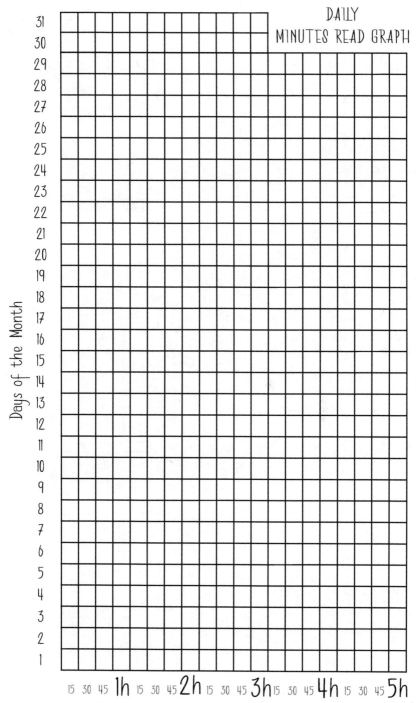

DAILY
MINUTES READ GRAPH

Days of the Month

31
30
29
28
27
26
25
24
23
22
21
20
19
18
17
16
15
14
13
12
11
10
9
8
7
6
5
4
3
2
1

15 30 45 1h 15 30 45 2h 15 30 45 3h 15 30 45 4h 15 30 45 5h

Minutes Read

July

JULY GOALS

_____

_____

_____

_____

BEST READS

_____

_____

_____

BEST BOOKS REVIEWED

_____

_____

_____

_____

_____

FAVORITE QUOTES

_____

_____

_____

_____

_____

_____

_____

Color one for every book you read in July.

Reading Minutes

DAILY MINUTES READ CHART

☐	MINUTES I WANT TO READ THIS MONTH
☐	ACTUAL MINUTES I READ THIS MONTH

1	2	3	4	5	6	7
8	9	10	11	12	13	14
15	16	17	18	19	20	21
22	23	24	25	26	27	28
29	30	31				

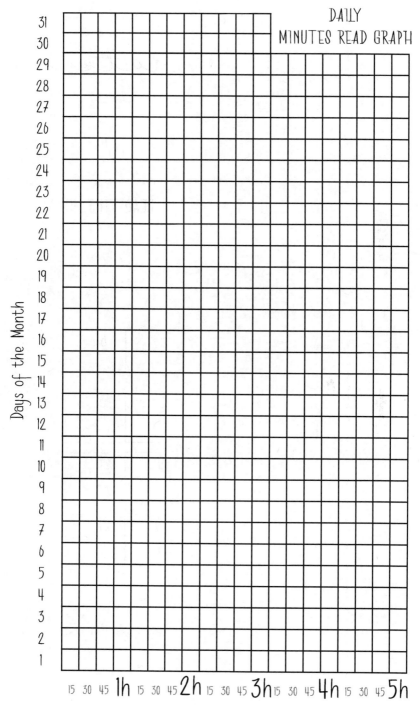

DAILY
MINUTES READ GRAPH

Days of the Month

31
30
29
28
27
26
25
24
23
22
21
20
19
18
17
16
15
14
13
12
11
10
9
8
7
6
5
4
3
2
1

15 30 45 **1h** 15 30 45 **2h** 15 30 45 **3h** 15 30 45 **4h** 15 30 45 **5h**

Minutes Read

August

AUGUST GOALS

_____

_____

_____

_____

BEST READS

_____

_____

_____

BEST BOOKS REVIEWED

_____

_____

_____

_____

_____

FAVORITE QUOTES

_____

_____

_____

_____

_____

_____

Color one for every book you read in August.

Reading Minutes

DAILY MINUTES READ CHART

☐	MINUTES I WANT TO READ THIS MONTH
☐	ACTUAL MINUTES I READ THIS MONTH

1	2	3	4	5	6	7
8	9	10	11	12	13	14
15	16	17	18	19	20	21
22	23	24	25	26	27	28
29	30	31				

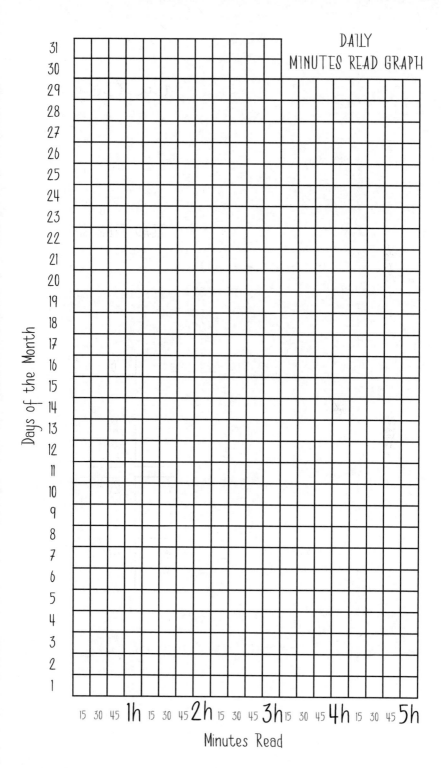

DAILY
MINUTES READ GRAPH

Days of the Month

31
30
29
28
27
26
25
24
23
22
21
20
19
18
17
16
15
14
13
12
11
10
9
8
7
6
5
4
3
2
1

15 30 45 1h 15 30 45 2h 15 30 45 3h 15 30 45 4h 15 30 45 5h

Minutes Read

September

SEPTEMBER GOALS

_____
_____
_____
_____

BEST READS

_____
_____
_____

BEST BOOKS REVIEWED

_____
_____
_____
_____
_____

FAVORITE QUOTES

_____

_____

_____

_____

_____

_____

_____

Color one for every book you read in September.

Reading Minutes

DAILY MINUTES READ CHART

☐	MINUTES I WANT TO READ THIS MONTH
☐	ACTUAL MINUTES I READ THIS MONTH

1	2	3	4	5	6	7
8	9	10	11	12	13	14
15	16	17	18	19	20	21
22	23	24	25	26	27	28
29	30	31				

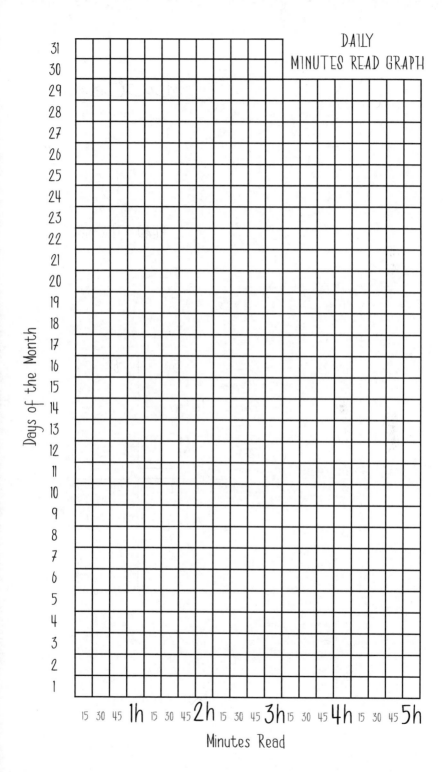

DAILY
MINUTES READ GRAPH

Days of the Month

31
30
29
28
27
26
25
24
23
22
21
20
19
18
17
16
15
14
13
12
11
10
9
8
7
6
5
4
3
2
1

15 30 45 **1h** 15 30 45 **2h** 15 30 45 **3h** 15 30 45 **4h** 15 30 45 **5h**

Minutes Read

October

OCTOBER GOALS

_____

_____

_____

_____

BEST READS

_____

_____

_____

BEST BOOKS REVIEWED

_____

_____

_____

_____

FAVORITE QUOTES

_____

_____

_____

_____

_____

_____

_____

Color one for every book you read in October.

Reading Minutes

DAILY MINUTES READ CHART

☐	MINUTES I WANT TO READ THIS MONTH
☐	ACTUAL MINUTES I READ THIS MONTH

1	2	3	4	5	6	7
8	9	10	11	12	13	14
15	16	17	18	19	20	21
22	23	24	25	26	27	28
29	30	31				

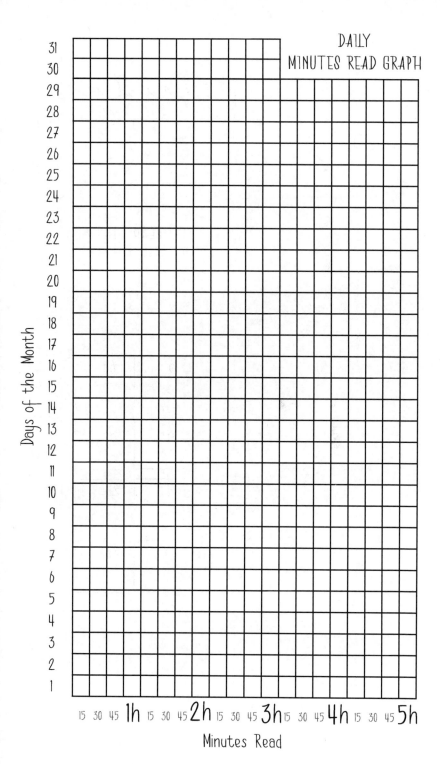

DAILY
MINUTES READ GRAPH

Days of the Month

31
30
29
28
27
26
25
24
23
22
21
20
19
18
17
16
15
14
13
12
11
10
9
8
7
6
5
4
3
2
1

15 30 45 **1h** 15 30 45 **2h** 15 30 45 **3h** 15 30 45 **4h** 15 30 45 **5h**

Minutes Read

November

NOVEMBER GOALS

_____

_____

_____

_____

BEST READS

_____

_____

_____

BEST BOOKS REVIEWED

_____

_____

_____

_____

_____

FAVORITE QUOTES

_____

_____

_____

_____

_____

_____

Color one for every book you read in November.

Reading Minutes

DAILY MINUTES READ CHART

☐	MINUTES I WANT TO READ THIS MONTH
☐	ACTUAL MINUTES I READ THIS MONTH

1	2	3	4	5	6	7
8	9	10	11	12	13	14
15	16	17	18	19	20	21
22	23	24	25	26	27	28
29	30	31				

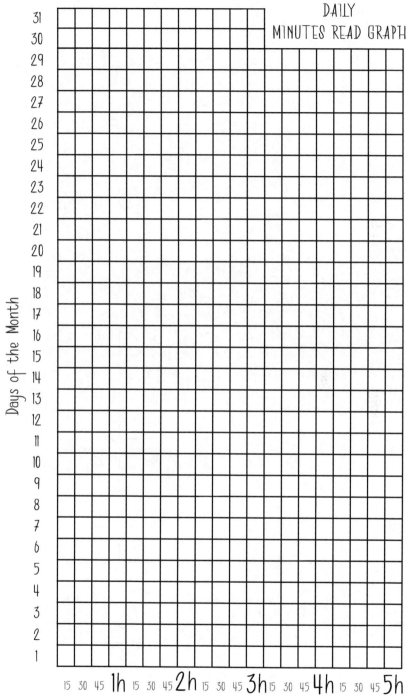

DAILY
MINUTES READ GRAPH

Days of the Month

31
30
29
28
27
26
25
24
23
22
21
20
19
18
17
16
15
14
13
12
11
10
9
8
7
6
5
4
3
2
1

15 30 45 **1h** 15 30 45 **2h** 15 30 45 **3h** 15 30 45 **4h** 15 30 45 **5h**

Minutes Read

December

DECEMBER GOALS

_____

_____

_____

_____

BEST READS

_____

_____

_____

BEST BOOKS REVIEWED

_____

_____

_____

_____

_____

FAVORITE QUOTES

_____

_____

_____

_____

_____

_____

Color one for every book you read in December.

Reading Minutes

DAILY MINUTES READ CHART

☐	MINUTES I WANT TO READ THIS MONTH
☐	ACTUAL MINUTES I READ THIS MONTH

1	2	3	4	5	6	7
8	9	10	11	12	13	14
15	16	17	18	19	20	21
22	23	24	25	26	27	28
29	30	31				

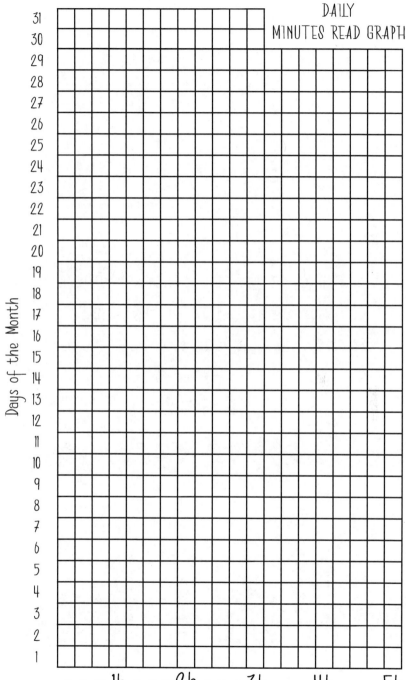

DAILY
MINUTES READ GRAPH

Days of the Month

31
30
29
28
27
26
25
24
23
22
21
20
19
18
17
16
15
14
13
12
11
10
9
8
7
6
5
4
3
2
1

15 30 45 **1h** 15 30 45 **2h** 15 30 45 **3h** 15 30 45 **4h** 15 30 45 **5h**

Minutes Read

Be diligent to present yourself
approved to God, a worker who
does not need to be ashamed,
rightly dividing the word of truth.

2 TIMOTHY 2 : 15

GIVE

THE GIFT OF STORIES

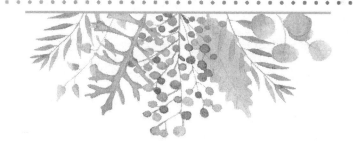

Books I've Been Given

_____

_____

_____

_____

_____

_____

_____

_____

_____

_____

_____

_____

_____

_____

_____

_____

_____

_____

_____

_____

Books I've Given

_____
_____
_____
_____
_____
_____

Books I Want to Give

_____
_____
_____
_____
_____
_____
_____
_____
_____
_____

Tell a Friend

If you liked

_____

. . . then you'll love

_____

If you liked

_____

. . . then you'll love

_____

If you liked

_____

. . . then you'll love

_____

If you liked

_____

. . . then you'll love

_____

Tell a Friend

If you liked

_____

... then you'll love

_____

* * * * * * * * * * * * * * * * * * * *

If you liked

_____

... then you'll love

_____

* * * * * * * * * * * * * * * * * * * *

If you liked

_____

... then you'll love

_____

* * * * * * * * * * * * * * * * * * * *

If you liked

_____

... then you'll love

_____

* * * * * * * * * * * * * * * * * * * *

Where are My Books?

_____

title

_____

borrower

_____   _____

date borrowed   date returned

_____

title

_____

borrower

_____   _____

date borrowed   date returned

_____

title

_____

borrower

_____   _____

date borrowed   date returned

Where are My Books?

_____
title

_____
borrower

_____   _____
date borrowed   date returned

_____
title

_____
borrower

_____   _____
date borrowed   date returned

_____
title

_____
borrower

_____   _____
date borrowed   date returned

Where are My Books?

_____

title

_____

borrower

_____   _____

date borrowed   date returned

_____

title

_____

borrower

_____   _____

date borrowed   date returned

_____

title

_____

borrower

_____   _____

date borrowed   date returned

Where are My Books?

_____

title

_____

borrower

_____   _____

date borrowed   date returned

_____

title

_____

borrower

_____   _____

date borrowed   date returned

_____

title

_____

borrower

_____   _____

date borrowed   date returned

Where are My Books?

_____

title

_____

borrower

_____   _____

date borrowed   date returned

_____

title

_____

borrower

_____   _____

date borrowed   date returned

_____

title

_____

borrower

_____   _____

date borrowed   date returned

Where are My Books?

_____

title

_____

borrower

_____   _____

date borrowed   date returned

_____

title

_____

borrower

_____   _____

date borrowed   date returned

_____

title

_____

borrower

_____   _____

date borrowed   date returned

Where are My Books?

_____

title

_____

borrower

_____   _____

date borrowed   date returned

_____

title

_____

borrower

_____   _____

date borrowed   date returned

_____

title

_____

borrower

_____   _____

date borrowed   date returned

Where are My Books?

_____

title

_____

borrower

_____   _____

date borrowed   date returned

_____

title

_____

borrower

_____   _____

date borrowed   date returned

_____

title

_____

borrower

_____   _____

date borrowed   date returned

Where are My Books?

_____

title

_____

borrower

_____   _____

date borrowed   date returned

_____

title

_____

borrower

_____   _____

date borrowed   date returned

_____

title

_____

borrower

_____   _____

date borrowed   date returned

Where are My Books?

_____

title

_____

borrower

_____   _____

date borrowed   date returned

_____

title

_____

borrower

_____   _____

date borrowed   date returned

_____

title

_____

borrower

_____   _____

date borrowed   date returned

Unfinished Books

_____
title

_____
author

_____

_____
reason abandoned

revisit?   [ ]   [ ]   [ ]
            Yes   No   Maybe

_____
title

_____
author

_____

_____
reason abandoned

revisit?   [ ]   [ ]   [ ]
            Yes   No   Maybe

Unfinished Books

_____

title

_____

author

_____

_____

reason abandoned

revisit? ☐ Yes   ☐ No   ☐ Maybe

_____

title

_____

author

_____

_____

reason abandoned

revisit? ☐ Yes   ☐ No   ☐ Maybe

Unfinished Books

_____

title

_____

author

_____

_____

reason abandoned

revisit? ☐ Yes   ☐ No   ☐ Maybe

_____

title

_____

author

_____

_____

reason abandoned

revisit? ☐ Yes   ☐ No   ☐ Maybe

Unfinished Books

_____

title

_____

author

_____

_____

reason abandoned

revisit?   [ ]   [ ]   [ ]
          Yes   No   Maybe

_____

title

_____

author

_____

_____

reason abandoned

revisit?   [ ]   [ ]   [ ]
          Yes   No   Maybe

Unfinished Books

_____

title

_____

author

_____

_____

reason abandoned

revisit? ☐   ☐   ☐
         Yes   No   Maybe

_____

title

_____

author

_____

_____

reason abandoned

revisit? ☐   ☐   ☐
         Yes   No   Maybe

Unfinished Books

_____

title

_____

author

_____

_____

reason abandoned

revisit? ☐ Yes   ☐ No   ☐ Maybe

_____

title

_____

author

_____

_____

reason abandoned

revisit? ☐ Yes   ☐ No   ☐ Maybe

Delight yourself in the Lord and
He will give you the desires of your heart.

PSALM 37 : 4

100 BOOKS

TRACKER & READING LOG

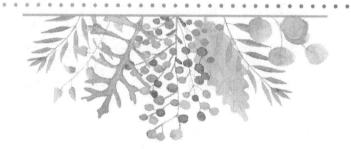

100 Book Challenge

100 Book Challenge

100 Book Challenge

100 Book Challenge

Reading Log

100 Book Challenge

☆ RATING

_____   _____

_____   _____

_____   _____

_____   _____

_____   _____

_____   _____

_____   _____

_____   _____

_____   _____

_____   _____

_____   _____

_____   _____

_____   _____

_____   _____

_____   _____

_____   _____

_____   _____

_____   _____

_____   _____

_____   _____

Reading Log

100 Book Challenge

☆ RATING

_____   _____

_____   _____

_____   _____

_____   _____

_____   _____

_____   _____

_____   _____

_____   _____

_____   _____

_____   _____

_____   _____

_____   _____

_____   _____

_____   _____

_____   _____

_____   _____

_____   _____

_____   _____

#41 - 60 Reading Log

100 Book Challenge

☆ RATING

_____ _____

_____ _____

_____ _____

_____ _____

_____ _____

_____ _____

_____ _____

_____ _____

_____ _____

_____ _____

_____ _____

_____ _____

_____ _____

_____ _____

_____ _____

_____ _____

_____ _____

_____ _____

Reading Log #61-80

100 Book Challenge

☆ RATING

_____ _____

_____ _____

_____ _____

_____ _____

_____ _____

_____ _____

_____ _____

_____ _____

_____ _____

_____ _____

_____ _____

_____ _____

_____ _____

_____ _____

_____ _____

_____ _____

_____ _____

_____ _____

_____ _____

_____ _____

81 - 100 Reading Log

100 Book Challenge

☆ RATING

Reading Log #101 - 120

100 Book Challenge

☆ RATING

Be strong and courageous. Do not be afraid or terrified because of them, for the Lord your God goes with you; he will never leave you nor forsake you.

DEUTERONOMY 31 : 6

REVIEWS

ORGANIZE YOUR THOUGHTS

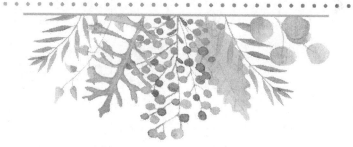

The Mark
OF A GREAT REVIEW

With a little help from Rel Mollet and Brenda S. Anderson,
here are some tips for writing great book reviews
(even if you didn't love the book).

DO craft an encouraging, truthful, and SHORT review

DON'T include spoilers

DO share about the story

DON'T rewrite the book description

DO say what you did and did not like

DON'T be insulting

DON'T give away the ending

Other things you might choose to include in a review include:

A moment of impact

Characters

Keywords for readers

(choose words that apply, such as page-turning, gripping,
unforgettable, mesmerizing, exceptional, authentic, well-written,
captivating, heart-warming, could not put down, a must-read)

Remember, **KEEP IT SHORT AND AVOID SPOILERS!**
Readers who are looking for their next read are not interested in
knowing all of the secrets ahead of time.

BOOK TITLE

Author

Genre

Date started   Date finished

REVIEW

RATING

Plot   ☆ ☆ ☆ ☆ ☆
Characters   ☆ ☆ ☆ ☆ ☆
Originality   ☆ ☆ ☆ ☆ ☆
Writing quality ☆ ☆ ☆ ☆ ☆
Overall   ☆ ☆ ☆ ☆ ☆

POSTED AT :

BOOK TITLE

Author

Genre

Date started   Date finished

REVIEW

RATING

Plot	☆	☆	☆	☆	☆
Characters	☆	☆	☆	☆	☆
Originality	☆	☆	☆	☆	☆
Writing quality	☆	☆	☆	☆	☆
Overall	☆	☆	☆	☆	☆

POSTED AT:

BOOK TITLE

Author

Genre

Date started   Date finished

REVIEW

_____

_____

_____

_____

_____

RATING

Plot   ☆ ☆ ☆ ☆ ☆
Characters   ☆ ☆ ☆ ☆ ☆
Originality   ☆ ☆ ☆ ☆ ☆
Writing quality ☆ ☆ ☆ ☆ ☆
Overall   ☆ ☆ ☆ ☆ ☆

POSTED AT:

_____

_____

_____

BOOK TITLE

Author

Genre

Date started   Date finished

REVIEW

_____

_____

_____

_____

RATING

Plot   ☆ ☆ ☆ ☆ ☆
Characters   ☆ ☆ ☆ ☆ ☆
Originality   ☆ ☆ ☆ ☆ ☆
Writing quality ☆ ☆ ☆ ☆ ☆
Overall   ☆ ☆ ☆ ☆ ☆

POSTED AT :

_____

_____

_____

BOOK TITLE

Author

Genre

Date started   Date finished

REVIEW

RATING

Plot	☆	☆	☆	☆	☆
Characters	☆	☆	☆	☆	☆
Originality	☆	☆	☆	☆	☆
Writing quality	☆	☆	☆	☆	☆
Overall	☆	☆	☆	☆	☆

POSTED AT :

BOOK TITLE

Author

Genre

Date started   Date finished

REVIEW

_____

_____

_____

_____

_____

RATING

Plot   ☆ ☆ ☆ ☆ ☆
Characters   ☆ ☆ ☆ ☆ ☆
Originality   ☆ ☆ ☆ ☆ ☆
Writing quality ☆ ☆ ☆ ☆ ☆
Overall   ☆ ☆ ☆ ☆ ☆

POSTED AT:

_____

_____

_____

BOOK TITLE

Author

Genre

Date started   Date finished

REVIEW

_____

_____

_____

_____

_____

RATING

Plot	☆	☆	☆	☆	☆
Characters	☆	☆	☆	☆	☆
Originality	☆	☆	☆	☆	☆
Writing quality	☆	☆	☆	☆	☆
Overall	☆	☆	☆	☆	☆

POSTED AT:

_____

_____

_____

BOOK TITLE

Author

Genre

Date started   Date finished

REVIEW

_____

_____

_____

_____

_____

RATING

Plot   ☆ ☆ ☆ ☆ ☆
Characters   ☆ ☆ ☆ ☆ ☆
Originality   ☆ ☆ ☆ ☆ ☆
Writing quality   ☆ ☆ ☆ ☆ ☆
Overall   ☆ ☆ ☆ ☆ ☆

POSTED AT :

_____

_____

_____

BOOK TITLE

Author

Genre

Date started   Date finished

REVIEW

RATING

Plot   ☆ ☆ ☆ ☆ ☆
Characters   ☆ ☆ ☆ ☆ ☆
Originality   ☆ ☆ ☆ ☆ ☆
Writing quality ☆ ☆ ☆ ☆ ☆
Overall   ☆ ☆ ☆ ☆ ☆

POSTED AT:

BOOK TITLE

Author

Genre

Date started   Date finished

REVIEW

RATING

Plot   ☆ ☆ ☆ ☆ ☆
Characters   ☆ ☆ ☆ ☆ ☆
Originality   ☆ ☆ ☆ ☆ ☆
Writing quality ☆ ☆ ☆ ☆ ☆
Overall   ☆ ☆ ☆ ☆ ☆

POSTED AT:

BOOK TITLE

Author

Genre

Date started   Date finished

REVIEW

RATING

Plot	☆ ☆ ☆ ☆ ☆
Characters	☆ ☆ ☆ ☆ ☆
Originality	☆ ☆ ☆ ☆ ☆
Writing quality	☆ ☆ ☆ ☆ ☆
Overall	☆ ☆ ☆ ☆ ☆

POSTED AT:

BOOK TITLE

Author

Genre

Date started   Date finished

REVIEW

RATING

Plot   ☆ ☆ ☆ ☆ ☆
Characters   ☆ ☆ ☆ ☆ ☆
Originality   ☆ ☆ ☆ ☆ ☆
Writing quality ☆ ☆ ☆ ☆ ☆
Overall   ☆ ☆ ☆ ☆ ☆

POSTED AT:

BOOK TITLE

Author

Genre

Date started   Date finished

REVIEW

_____

_____

_____

_____

_____

RATING

Plot   ☆ ☆ ☆ ☆ ☆
Characters   ☆ ☆ ☆ ☆ ☆
Originality   ☆ ☆ ☆ ☆ ☆
Writing quality ☆ ☆ ☆ ☆ ☆
Overall   ☆ ☆ ☆ ☆ ☆

POSTED AT:

_____

_____

_____

BOOK TITLE

Author

Genre

Date started   Date finished

REVIEW

RATING

Plot   ☆ ☆ ☆ ☆ ☆
Characters   ☆ ☆ ☆ ☆ ☆
Originality   ☆ ☆ ☆ ☆ ☆
Writing quality ☆ ☆ ☆ ☆ ☆
Overall   ☆ ☆ ☆ ☆ ☆

POSTED AT :

BOOK TITLE

Author

Genre

Date started   Date finished

REVIEW

RATING

Plot   ☆ ☆ ☆ ☆ ☆
Characters   ☆ ☆ ☆ ☆ ☆
Originality   ☆ ☆ ☆ ☆ ☆
Writing quality ☆ ☆ ☆ ☆ ☆
Overall   ☆ ☆ ☆ ☆ ☆

POSTED AT :

BOOK TITLE

Author

Genre

Date started   Date finished

REVIEW

_____

_____

_____

_____

_____

RATING

Plot	☆	☆	☆	☆	☆
Characters	☆	☆	☆	☆	☆
Originality	☆	☆	☆	☆	☆
Writing quality	☆	☆	☆	☆	☆
Overall	☆	☆	☆	☆	☆

POSTED AT:

_____

_____

_____

BOOK TITLE

Author

Genre

Date started   Date finished

REVIEW

_____

_____

_____

_____

_____

RATING

Plot   ☆ ☆ ☆ ☆ ☆
Characters   ☆ ☆ ☆ ☆ ☆
Originality   ☆ ☆ ☆ ☆ ☆
Writing quality ☆ ☆ ☆ ☆ ☆
Overall   ☆ ☆ ☆ ☆ ☆

POSTED AT:

_____

_____

_____

BOOK TITLE

Author

Genre

Date started   Date finished

REVIEW

_____

_____

_____

_____

_____

RATING

Plot   ☆ ☆ ☆ ☆ ☆
Characters   ☆ ☆ ☆ ☆ ☆
Originality   ☆ ☆ ☆ ☆ ☆
Writing quality ☆ ☆ ☆ ☆ ☆
Overall   ☆ ☆ ☆ ☆ ☆

POSTED AT:

_____

_____

_____

BOOK TITLE

Author

Genre

Date started   Date finished

REVIEW

RATING

Plot   ☆ ☆ ☆ ☆ ☆
Characters   ☆ ☆ ☆ ☆ ☆
Originality   ☆ ☆ ☆ ☆ ☆
Writing quality ☆ ☆ ☆ ☆ ☆
Overall   ☆ ☆ ☆ ☆ ☆

POSTED AT:

BOOK TITLE

Author

Genre

Date started   Date finished

REVIEW

_____

_____

_____

_____

_____

RATING

Plot   ☆ ☆ ☆ ☆ ☆
Characters   ☆ ☆ ☆ ☆ ☆
Originality   ☆ ☆ ☆ ☆ ☆
Writing quality   ☆ ☆ ☆ ☆ ☆
Overall   ☆ ☆ ☆ ☆ ☆

POSTED AT :

_____

_____

_____

BOOK TITLE

Author

Genre

Date started   Date finished

REVIEW

_____

_____

_____

_____

_____

RATING

Plot   ☆ ☆ ☆ ☆ ☆
Characters   ☆ ☆ ☆ ☆ ☆
Originality   ☆ ☆ ☆ ☆ ☆
Writing quality   ☆ ☆ ☆ ☆ ☆
Overall   ☆ ☆ ☆ ☆ ☆

POSTED AT:

_____

_____

_____

BOOK TITLE

Author

Genre

Date started   Date finished

REVIEW

_____

_____

_____

_____

_____

RATING

Plot	☆ ☆ ☆ ☆ ☆
Characters	☆ ☆ ☆ ☆ ☆
Originality	☆ ☆ ☆ ☆ ☆
Writing quality	☆ ☆ ☆ ☆ ☆
Overall	☆ ☆ ☆ ☆ ☆

POSTED AT:

_____

_____

_____

BOOK TITLE

Author

Genre

Date started   Date finished

REVIEW

_____

_____

_____

_____

_____

RATING

Plot   ☆ ☆ ☆ ☆ ☆
Characters   ☆ ☆ ☆ ☆ ☆
Originality   ☆ ☆ ☆ ☆ ☆
Writing quality ☆ ☆ ☆ ☆ ☆
Overall   ☆ ☆ ☆ ☆ ☆

POSTED AT:

_____

_____

_____

BOOK TITLE

Author

Genre

Date started   Date finished

REVIEW

RATING

Plot	☆	☆	☆	☆	☆
Characters	☆	☆	☆	☆	☆
Originality	☆	☆	☆	☆	☆
Writing quality	☆	☆	☆	☆	☆
Overall	☆	☆	☆	☆	☆

POSTED AT:

BOOK TITLE

Author

Genre

Date started   Date finished

REVIEW

_____

_____

_____

_____

_____

RATING

Plot   ☆ ☆ ☆ ☆ ☆
Characters   ☆ ☆ ☆ ☆ ☆
Originality   ☆ ☆ ☆ ☆ ☆
Writing quality ☆ ☆ ☆ ☆ ☆
Overall   ☆ ☆ ☆ ☆ ☆

POSTED AT :

_____

_____

_____

BOOK TITLE

Author

Genre

Date started   Date finished

REVIEW

_____

_____

_____

_____

_____

RATING

Plot   ☆ ☆ ☆ ☆ ☆
Characters   ☆ ☆ ☆ ☆ ☆
Originality   ☆ ☆ ☆ ☆ ☆
Writing quality ☆ ☆ ☆ ☆ ☆
Overall   ☆ ☆ ☆ ☆ ☆

POSTED AT:

_____

_____

_____

BOOK TITLE

Author

Genre

Date started   Date finished

REVIEW

_____

_____

_____

_____

_____

RATING

Plot   ☆ ☆ ☆ ☆ ☆
Characters   ☆ ☆ ☆ ☆ ☆
Originality   ☆ ☆ ☆ ☆ ☆
Writing quality ☆ ☆ ☆ ☆ ☆
Overall   ☆ ☆ ☆ ☆ ☆

POSTED AT:

_____

_____

_____

BOOK TITLE

Author

Genre

Date started   Date finished

REVIEW

_____

_____

_____

_____

_____

RATING

Plot   ☆ ☆ ☆ ☆ ☆
Characters   ☆ ☆ ☆ ☆ ☆
Originality   ☆ ☆ ☆ ☆ ☆
Writing quality ☆ ☆ ☆ ☆ ☆
Overall   ☆ ☆ ☆ ☆ ☆

POSTED AT :

_____

_____

_____

BOOK TITLE

Author

Genre

Date started   Date finished

REVIEW

_____

_____

_____

_____

_____

RATING

Plot	☆	☆	☆	☆	☆
Characters	☆	☆	☆	☆	☆
Originality	☆	☆	☆	☆	☆
Writing quality	☆	☆	☆	☆	☆
Overall	☆	☆	☆	☆	☆

POSTED AT:

_____

_____

_____

BOOK TITLE

Author

Genre

Date started   Date finished

REVIEW

RATING

Plot	☆ ☆ ☆ ☆ ☆
Characters	☆ ☆ ☆ ☆ ☆
Originality	☆ ☆ ☆ ☆ ☆
Writing quality	☆ ☆ ☆ ☆ ☆
Overall	☆ ☆ ☆ ☆ ☆

POSTED AT :

BOOK TITLE

Author

Genre

Date started   Date finished

REVIEW

_____

_____

_____

_____

_____

RATING

Plot   ☆ ☆ ☆ ☆ ☆
Characters   ☆ ☆ ☆ ☆ ☆
Originality   ☆ ☆ ☆ ☆ ☆
Writing quality   ☆ ☆ ☆ ☆ ☆
Overall   ☆ ☆ ☆ ☆ ☆

POSTED AT:

_____

_____

_____

BOOK TITLE

Author

Genre

Date started   Date finished

REVIEW

_____

_____

_____

_____

_____

RATING

Plot	☆	☆	☆	☆	☆
Characters	☆	☆	☆	☆	☆
Originality	☆	☆	☆	☆	☆
Writing quality	☆	☆	☆	☆	☆
Overall	☆	☆	☆	☆	☆

POSTED AT:

_____

_____

_____

BOOK TITLE

Author

Genre

Date started   Date finished

REVIEW

_____

_____

_____

_____

_____

RATING

Plot	☆ ☆ ☆ ☆ ☆
Characters	☆ ☆ ☆ ☆ ☆
Originality	☆ ☆ ☆ ☆ ☆
Writing quality	☆ ☆ ☆ ☆ ☆
Overall	☆ ☆ ☆ ☆ ☆

POSTED AT :

_____

_____

_____

BOOK TITLE

Author

Genre

Date started   Date finished

REVIEW

_____

_____

_____

_____

_____

RATING

Plot	☆	☆	☆	☆	☆
Characters	☆	☆	☆	☆	☆
Originality	☆	☆	☆	☆	☆
Writing quality	☆	☆	☆	☆	☆
Overall	☆	☆	☆	☆	☆

POSTED AT:

_____

_____

_____

BOOK TITLE

Author

Genre

Date started   Date finished

REVIEW

_____

_____

_____

_____

_____

RATING

Plot	☆	☆	☆	☆	☆
Characters	☆	☆	☆	☆	☆
Originality	☆	☆	☆	☆	☆
Writing quality	☆	☆	☆	☆	☆
Overall	☆	☆	☆	☆	☆

POSTED AT:

_____

_____

_____

BOOK TITLE

Author

Genre

Date started   Date finished

REVIEW

_____

_____

_____

_____

_____

RATING

Plot   ☆ ☆ ☆ ☆ ☆
Characters   ☆ ☆ ☆ ☆ ☆
Originality   ☆ ☆ ☆ ☆ ☆
Writing quality ☆ ☆ ☆ ☆ ☆
Overall   ☆ ☆ ☆ ☆ ☆

POSTED AT:

_____

_____

_____

BOOK TITLE

Author

Genre

Date started   Date finished

REVIEW

RATING

Plot   ☆ ☆ ☆ ☆ ☆
Characters   ☆ ☆ ☆ ☆ ☆
Originality   ☆ ☆ ☆ ☆ ☆
Writing quality ☆ ☆ ☆ ☆ ☆
Overall   ☆ ☆ ☆ ☆ ☆

POSTED AT:

BOOK TITLE

Author

Genre

Date started   Date finished

REVIEW

_____

_____

_____

_____

_____

RATING

Plot	☆ ☆ ☆ ☆ ☆
Characters	☆ ☆ ☆ ☆ ☆
Originality	☆ ☆ ☆ ☆ ☆
Writing quality	☆ ☆ ☆ ☆ ☆
Overall	☆ ☆ ☆ ☆ ☆

POSTED AT:

_____

_____

_____

BOOK TITLE

Author

Genre

Date started   Date finished

REVIEW

_____

_____

_____

_____

_____

RATING

Plot   ☆ ☆ ☆ ☆ ☆
Characters   ☆ ☆ ☆ ☆ ☆
Originality   ☆ ☆ ☆ ☆ ☆
Writing quality ☆ ☆ ☆ ☆ ☆
Overall   ☆ ☆ ☆ ☆ ☆

POSTED AT :

_____

_____

_____

BOOK TITLE

Author _____

Genre _____

Date started _____ Date finished _____

REVIEW

_____
_____
_____
_____
_____

RATING

Plot	☆	☆	☆	☆	☆
Characters	☆	☆	☆	☆	☆
Originality	☆	☆	☆	☆	☆
Writing quality	☆	☆	☆	☆	☆
Overall	☆	☆	☆	☆	☆

POSTED AT:

_____
_____
_____

BOOK TITLE

Author

Genre

Date started   Date finished

REVIEW

_____

_____

_____

_____

_____

RATING

Plot   ☆ ☆ ☆ ☆ ☆
Characters   ☆ ☆ ☆ ☆ ☆
Originality   ☆ ☆ ☆ ☆ ☆
Writing quality   ☆ ☆ ☆ ☆ ☆
Overall   ☆ ☆ ☆ ☆ ☆

POSTED AT :

_____

_____

_____

BOOK TITLE

Author

Genre

Date started   Date finished

REVIEW

_____

_____

_____

_____

_____

RATING

Plot	☆	☆	☆	☆	☆
Characters	☆	☆	☆	☆	☆
Originality	☆	☆	☆	☆	☆
Writing quality	☆	☆	☆	☆	☆
Overall	☆	☆	☆	☆	☆

POSTED AT :

_____

_____

_____

BOOK TITLE

Author

Genre

Date started   Date finished

REVIEW

_____

_____

_____

_____

_____

RATING

Plot   ☆ ☆ ☆ ☆ ☆
Characters   ☆ ☆ ☆ ☆ ☆
Originality   ☆ ☆ ☆ ☆ ☆
Writing quality ☆ ☆ ☆ ☆ ☆
Overall   ☆ ☆ ☆ ☆ ☆

POSTED AT:

_____

_____

_____

BOOK TITLE

Author

Genre

Date started   Date finished

REVIEW

RATING

Plot	☆	☆	☆	☆	☆
Characters	☆	☆	☆	☆	☆
Originality	☆	☆	☆	☆	☆
Writing quality	☆	☆	☆	☆	☆
Overall	☆	☆	☆	☆	☆

POSTED AT:

BOOK TITLE

Author

Genre

Date started   Date finished

REVIEW

_____

_____

_____

_____

_____

RATING

Plot   ☆ ☆ ☆ ☆ ☆
Characters   ☆ ☆ ☆ ☆ ☆
Originality   ☆ ☆ ☆ ☆ ☆
Writing quality ☆ ☆ ☆ ☆ ☆
Overall   ☆ ☆ ☆ ☆ ☆

POSTED AT:

_____

_____

_____

BOOK TITLE

Author

Genre

Date started   Date finished

REVIEW

_____

_____

_____

_____

_____

RATING

Plot	☆ ☆ ☆ ☆ ☆
Characters	☆ ☆ ☆ ☆ ☆
Originality	☆ ☆ ☆ ☆ ☆
Writing quality	☆ ☆ ☆ ☆ ☆
Overall	☆ ☆ ☆ ☆ ☆

POSTED AT:

_____

_____

_____

BOOK TITLE

Author

Genre

Date started   Date finished

REVIEW

_____

_____

_____

_____

_____

RATING

Plot	☆	☆	☆	☆	☆
Characters	☆	☆	☆	☆	☆
Originality	☆	☆	☆	☆	☆
Writing quality	☆	☆	☆	☆	☆
Overall	☆	☆	☆	☆	☆

POSTED AT:

_____

_____

_____

BOOK TITLE

Author

Genre

Date started   Date finished

REVIEW

_____

_____

_____

_____

_____

RATING

Plot	☆	☆	☆	☆	☆
Characters	☆	☆	☆	☆	☆
Originality	☆	☆	☆	☆	☆
Writing quality	☆	☆	☆	☆	☆
Overall	☆	☆	☆	☆	☆

POSTED AT:

_____

_____

_____

BOOK TITLE

Author

Genre

Date started   Date finished

REVIEW

_____

_____

_____

_____

_____

RATING

Plot   ☆ ☆ ☆ ☆ ☆
Characters   ☆ ☆ ☆ ☆ ☆
Originality   ☆ ☆ ☆ ☆ ☆
Writing quality ☆ ☆ ☆ ☆ ☆
Overall   ☆ ☆ ☆ ☆ ☆

POSTED AT:

_____

_____

_____

BOOK TITLE

Author

Genre

Date started   Date finished

REVIEW

_____

_____

_____

_____

_____

RATING

Plot   ☆ ☆ ☆ ☆ ☆
Characters   ☆ ☆ ☆ ☆ ☆
Originality   ☆ ☆ ☆ ☆ ☆
Writing quality ☆ ☆ ☆ ☆ ☆
Overall   ☆ ☆ ☆ ☆ ☆

POSTED AT :

_____

_____

_____

BOOK TITLE

Author

Genre

Date started   Date finished

REVIEW

_____

_____

_____

_____

_____

RATING

Plot	☆	☆	☆	☆	☆
Characters	☆	☆	☆	☆	☆
Originality	☆	☆	☆	☆	☆
Writing quality	☆	☆	☆	☆	☆
Overall	☆	☆	☆	☆	☆

POSTED AT :

_____

_____

_____

BOOK TITLE

Author

Genre

Date started   Date finished

REVIEW

_____

_____

_____

_____

_____

RATING

Plot   ☆ ☆ ☆ ☆ ☆
Characters   ☆ ☆ ☆ ☆ ☆
Originality   ☆ ☆ ☆ ☆ ☆
Writing quality   ☆ ☆ ☆ ☆ ☆
Overall   ☆ ☆ ☆ ☆ ☆

POSTED AT :

_____

_____

_____

BOOK TITLE

Author _____

Genre _____

Date started _____ Date finished _____

REVIEW

_____

_____

_____

_____

_____

RATING

Plot   ☆ ☆ ☆ ☆ ☆
Characters   ☆ ☆ ☆ ☆ ☆
Originality   ☆ ☆ ☆ ☆ ☆
Writing quality ☆ ☆ ☆ ☆ ☆
Overall   ☆ ☆ ☆ ☆ ☆

POSTED AT:

_____

_____

_____

BOOK TITLE

Author

Genre

Date started   Date finished

REVIEW

_____

_____

_____

_____

_____

RATING

Plot   ☆ ☆ ☆ ☆ ☆
Characters   ☆ ☆ ☆ ☆ ☆
Originality   ☆ ☆ ☆ ☆ ☆
Writing quality   ☆ ☆ ☆ ☆ ☆
Overall   ☆ ☆ ☆ ☆ ☆

POSTED AT :

_____

_____

_____

BOOK TITLE

Author

Genre

Date started   Date finished

REVIEW

_____

_____

_____

_____

_____

RATING

Plot	☆	☆	☆	☆	☆
Characters	☆	☆	☆	☆	☆
Originality	☆	☆	☆	☆	☆
Writing quality	☆	☆	☆	☆	☆
Overall	☆	☆	☆	☆	☆

POSTED AT:

_____

_____

_____

BOOK TITLE

Author

Genre

Date started   Date finished

REVIEW

_____

_____

_____

_____

_____

RATING

Plot   ☆ ☆ ☆ ☆ ☆
Characters   ☆ ☆ ☆ ☆ ☆
Originality   ☆ ☆ ☆ ☆ ☆
Writing quality ☆ ☆ ☆ ☆ ☆
Overall   ☆ ☆ ☆ ☆ ☆

POSTED AT :

_____

_____

_____

BOOK TITLE

Author

Genre

Date started   Date finished

REVIEW

_____

_____

_____

_____

_____

RATING

Plot   ☆ ☆ ☆ ☆ ☆
Characters   ☆ ☆ ☆ ☆ ☆
Originality   ☆ ☆ ☆ ☆ ☆
Writing quality ☆ ☆ ☆ ☆ ☆
Overall   ☆ ☆ ☆ ☆ ☆

POSTED AT :

_____

_____

_____

BOOK TITLE

Author

Genre

Date started   Date finished

REVIEW

_____

_____

_____

_____

_____

RATING

Plot   ☆ ☆ ☆ ☆ ☆
Characters   ☆ ☆ ☆ ☆ ☆
Originality   ☆ ☆ ☆ ☆ ☆
Writing quality   ☆ ☆ ☆ ☆ ☆
Overall   ☆ ☆ ☆ ☆ ☆

POSTED AT:

_____

_____

_____

BOOK TITLE

Author

Genre

Date started   Date finished

REVIEW

_____

_____

_____

_____

_____

RATING

Plot	☆	☆	☆	☆	☆
Characters	☆	☆	☆	☆	☆
Originality	☆	☆	☆	☆	☆
Writing quality	☆	☆	☆	☆	☆
Overall	☆	☆	☆	☆	☆

POSTED AT:

_____

_____

_____

BOOK TITLE

Author

Genre

Date started   Date finished

REVIEW

_____

_____

_____

_____

_____

RATING

Plot	☆	☆	☆	☆	☆
Characters	☆	☆	☆	☆	☆
Originality	☆	☆	☆	☆	☆
Writing quality	☆	☆	☆	☆	☆
Overall	☆	☆	☆	☆	☆

POSTED AT :

_____

_____

_____

BOOK TITLE

Author

Genre

Date started   Date finished

REVIEW

_____

_____

_____

_____

_____

RATING

Plot   ☆ ☆ ☆ ☆ ☆
Characters   ☆ ☆ ☆ ☆ ☆
Originality   ☆ ☆ ☆ ☆ ☆
Writing quality   ☆ ☆ ☆ ☆ ☆
Overall   ☆ ☆ ☆ ☆ ☆

POSTED AT:

_____

_____

_____

BOOK TITLE

Author

Genre

Date started   Date finished

REVIEW

_____

_____

_____

_____

_____

RATING

Plot   ☆ ☆ ☆ ☆ ☆
Characters   ☆ ☆ ☆ ☆ ☆
Originality   ☆ ☆ ☆ ☆ ☆
Writing quality ☆ ☆ ☆ ☆ ☆
Overall   ☆ ☆ ☆ ☆ ☆

POSTED AT :

_____

_____

_____

BOOK TITLE

Author

Genre

Date started   Date finished

REVIEW

RATING

Plot   ☆ ☆ ☆ ☆ ☆
Characters   ☆ ☆ ☆ ☆ ☆
Originality   ☆ ☆ ☆ ☆ ☆
Writing quality ☆ ☆ ☆ ☆ ☆
Overall   ☆ ☆ ☆ ☆ ☆

POSTED AT :

BOOK TITLE

Author

Genre

Date started   Date finished

REVIEW

_____

_____

_____

_____

_____

RATING

Plot   ☆ ☆ ☆ ☆ ☆
Characters   ☆ ☆ ☆ ☆ ☆
Originality   ☆ ☆ ☆ ☆ ☆
Writing quality ☆ ☆ ☆ ☆ ☆
Overall   ☆ ☆ ☆ ☆ ☆

POSTED AT :

_____

_____

_____

BOOK TITLE

Author

Genre

Date started   Date finished

REVIEW

_____

_____

_____

_____

_____

RATING

Plot	☆	☆	☆	☆	☆
Characters	☆	☆	☆	☆	☆
Originality	☆	☆	☆	☆	☆
Writing quality	☆	☆	☆	☆	☆
Overall	☆	☆	☆	☆	☆

POSTED AT :

_____

_____

_____

BOOK TITLE

Author

Genre

Date started   Date finished

REVIEW

RATING

Plot   ☆ ☆ ☆ ☆ ☆
Characters   ☆ ☆ ☆ ☆ ☆
Originality   ☆ ☆ ☆ ☆ ☆
Writing quality ☆ ☆ ☆ ☆ ☆
Overall   ☆ ☆ ☆ ☆ ☆

POSTED AT:

BOOK TITLE

Author

Genre

Date started   Date finished

REVIEW

_____

_____

_____

_____

_____

RATING

Plot   ☆ ☆ ☆ ☆ ☆
Characters   ☆ ☆ ☆ ☆ ☆
Originality   ☆ ☆ ☆ ☆ ☆
Writing quality ☆ ☆ ☆ ☆ ☆
Overall   ☆ ☆ ☆ ☆ ☆

POSTED AT:

_____

_____

_____

BOOK TITLE

Author

Genre

Date started   Date finished

REVIEW

_____

_____

_____

_____

_____

RATING

Plot   ☆ ☆ ☆ ☆ ☆
Characters   ☆ ☆ ☆ ☆ ☆
Originality   ☆ ☆ ☆ ☆ ☆
Writing quality ☆ ☆ ☆ ☆ ☆
Overall   ☆ ☆ ☆ ☆ ☆

POSTED AT:

_____

_____

_____

BOOK TITLE

Author

Genre

Date started   Date finished

REVIEW

_____

_____

_____

_____

_____

RATING

Plot	☆ ☆ ☆ ☆ ☆
Characters	☆ ☆ ☆ ☆ ☆
Originality	☆ ☆ ☆ ☆ ☆
Writing quality	☆ ☆ ☆ ☆ ☆
Overall	☆ ☆ ☆ ☆ ☆

POSTED AT:

_____

_____

_____

BOOK TITLE

Author

Genre

Date started   Date finished

REVIEW

_____

_____

_____

_____

_____

RATING

Plot	☆ ☆ ☆ ☆ ☆	
Characters	☆ ☆ ☆ ☆ ☆	
Originality	☆ ☆ ☆ ☆ ☆	
Writing quality	☆ ☆ ☆ ☆ ☆	
Overall	☆ ☆ ☆ ☆ ☆	

POSTED AT:

_____

_____

_____

BOOK TITLE

Author

Genre

Date started   Date finished

REVIEW

_____

_____

_____

_____

_____

RATING

Plot	☆	☆	☆	☆	☆
Characters	☆	☆	☆	☆	☆
Originality	☆	☆	☆	☆	☆
Writing quality	☆	☆	☆	☆	☆
Overall	☆	☆	☆	☆	☆

POSTED AT :

_____

_____

_____

BOOK TITLE

Author

Genre

Date started   Date finished

REVIEW

_____

_____

_____

_____

_____

RATING

Plot   ☆ ☆ ☆ ☆ ☆
Characters   ☆ ☆ ☆ ☆ ☆
Originality   ☆ ☆ ☆ ☆ ☆
Writing quality ☆ ☆ ☆ ☆ ☆
Overall   ☆ ☆ ☆ ☆ ☆

POSTED AT :

_____

_____

_____

BOOK TITLE

Author

Genre

Date started   Date finished

REVIEW

_____

_____

_____

_____

_____

RATING

Plot   ☆ ☆ ☆ ☆ ☆
Characters   ☆ ☆ ☆ ☆ ☆
Originality   ☆ ☆ ☆ ☆ ☆
Writing quality ☆ ☆ ☆ ☆ ☆
Overall   ☆ ☆ ☆ ☆ ☆

POSTED AT :

_____

_____

_____

BOOK TITLE

Author

Genre

Date started   Date finished

REVIEW

_____

_____

_____

_____

_____

RATING

Plot   ☆ ☆ ☆ ☆ ☆
Characters   ☆ ☆ ☆ ☆ ☆
Originality   ☆ ☆ ☆ ☆ ☆
Writing quality ☆ ☆ ☆ ☆ ☆
Overall   ☆ ☆ ☆ ☆ ☆

POSTED AT:

_____

_____

_____

BOOK TITLE

Author

Genre

Date started   Date finished

REVIEW

_____

_____

_____

_____

_____

RATING

Plot	☆	☆	☆	☆	☆
Characters	☆	☆	☆	☆	☆
Originality	☆	☆	☆	☆	☆
Writing quality	☆	☆	☆	☆	☆
Overall	☆	☆	☆	☆	☆

POSTED AT :

_____

_____

_____

BOOK TITLE

Author

Genre

Date started   Date finished

REVIEW

_____

_____

_____

_____

_____

RATING

Plot   ☆ ☆ ☆ ☆ ☆
Characters   ☆ ☆ ☆ ☆ ☆
Originality   ☆ ☆ ☆ ☆ ☆
Writing quality ☆ ☆ ☆ ☆ ☆
Overall   ☆ ☆ ☆ ☆ ☆

POSTED AT:

_____

_____

_____

BOOK TITLE

Author

Genre

Date started   Date finished

REVIEW

_____

_____

_____

_____

_____

RATING

Plot   ☆ ☆ ☆ ☆ ☆
Characters   ☆ ☆ ☆ ☆ ☆
Originality   ☆ ☆ ☆ ☆ ☆
Writing quality ☆ ☆ ☆ ☆ ☆
Overall   ☆ ☆ ☆ ☆ ☆

POSTED AT:

_____

_____

_____

BOOK TITLE

Author

Genre

Date started   Date finished

REVIEW

_____

_____

_____

_____

_____

RATING

Plot	☆	☆	☆	☆	☆
Characters	☆	☆	☆	☆	☆
Originality	☆	☆	☆	☆	☆
Writing quality	☆	☆	☆	☆	☆
Overall	☆	☆	☆	☆	☆

POSTED AT:

_____

_____

_____

BOOK TITLE

Author

Genre

Date started   Date finished

REVIEW

_____

_____

_____

_____

_____

RATING

Plot	☆	☆	☆	☆	☆
Characters	☆	☆	☆	☆	☆
Originality	☆	☆	☆	☆	☆
Writing quality	☆	☆	☆	☆	☆
Overall	☆	☆	☆	☆	☆

POSTED AT :

_____

_____

_____

BOOK TITLE

Author

Genre

Date started   Date finished

REVIEW

_____

_____

_____

_____

_____

RATING

Plot	☆	☆	☆	☆	☆
Characters	☆	☆	☆	☆	☆
Originality	☆	☆	☆	☆	☆
Writing quality	☆	☆	☆	☆	☆
Overall	☆	☆	☆	☆	☆

POSTED AT:

_____

_____

_____

BOOK TITLE

Author

Genre

Date started   Date finished

REVIEW

_____

_____

_____

_____

_____

RATING

Plot	☆	☆	☆	☆	☆
Characters	☆	☆	☆	☆	☆
Originality	☆	☆	☆	☆	☆
Writing quality	☆	☆	☆	☆	☆
Overall	☆	☆	☆	☆	☆

POSTED AT :

_____

_____

_____

BOOK TITLE

Author

Genre

Date started   Date finished

REVIEW

_____

_____

_____

_____

_____

RATING

Plot   ☆ ☆ ☆ ☆ ☆
Characters   ☆ ☆ ☆ ☆ ☆
Originality   ☆ ☆ ☆ ☆ ☆
Writing quality ☆ ☆ ☆ ☆ ☆
Overall   ☆ ☆ ☆ ☆ ☆

POSTED AT :

_____

_____

_____

BOOK TITLE

Author

Genre

Date started   Date finished

REVIEW

_____

_____

_____

_____

_____

RATING

Plot   ☆ ☆ ☆ ☆ ☆
Characters   ☆ ☆ ☆ ☆ ☆
Originality   ☆ ☆ ☆ ☆ ☆
Writing quality   ☆ ☆ ☆ ☆ ☆
Overall   ☆ ☆ ☆ ☆ ☆

POSTED AT :

_____

_____

_____

BOOK TITLE

Author

Genre

Date started   Date finished

REVIEW

_____

_____

_____

_____

_____

RATING

Plot   ☆ ☆ ☆ ☆ ☆
Characters   ☆ ☆ ☆ ☆ ☆
Originality   ☆ ☆ ☆ ☆ ☆
Writing quality ☆ ☆ ☆ ☆ ☆
Overall   ☆ ☆ ☆ ☆ ☆

POSTED AT:

_____

_____

_____

BOOK TITLE

Author

Genre

Date started   Date finished

REVIEW

_____

_____

_____

_____

_____

RATING

Plot   ☆ ☆ ☆ ☆ ☆
Characters   ☆ ☆ ☆ ☆ ☆
Originality   ☆ ☆ ☆ ☆ ☆
Writing quality ☆ ☆ ☆ ☆ ☆
Overall   ☆ ☆ ☆ ☆ ☆

POSTED AT:

_____

_____

_____

BOOK TITLE

Author

Genre

Date started   Date finished

REVIEW

RATING

Plot	☆	☆	☆	☆	☆
Characters	☆	☆	☆	☆	☆
Originality	☆	☆	☆	☆	☆
Writing quality	☆	☆	☆	☆	☆
Overall	☆	☆	☆	☆	☆

POSTED AT:

BOOK TITLE

Author

Genre

Date started   Date finished

REVIEW

_____

_____

_____

_____

_____

RATING

Plot	☆	☆	☆	☆	☆
Characters	☆	☆	☆	☆	☆
Originality	☆	☆	☆	☆	☆
Writing quality	☆	☆	☆	☆	☆
Overall	☆	☆	☆	☆	☆

POSTED AT :

_____

_____

_____

BOOK TITLE

Author

Genre

Date started

Date finished

REVIEW

RATING

Plot	☆	☆	☆	☆	☆
Characters	☆	☆	☆	☆	☆
Originality	☆	☆	☆	☆	☆
Writing quality	☆	☆	☆	☆	☆
Overall	☆	☆	☆	☆	☆

POSTED AT :

BOOK TITLE

Author

Genre

Date started   Date finished

REVIEW

RATING

Plot	☆ ☆ ☆ ☆ ☆
Characters	☆ ☆ ☆ ☆ ☆
Originality	☆ ☆ ☆ ☆ ☆
Writing quality	☆ ☆ ☆ ☆ ☆
Overall	☆ ☆ ☆ ☆ ☆

POSTED AT :

BOOK TITLE

Author _____

Genre _____

Date started _____ Date finished _____

REVIEW

_____

_____

_____

_____

_____

RATING

Plot	☆	☆	☆	☆	☆
Characters	☆	☆	☆	☆	☆
Originality	☆	☆	☆	☆	☆
Writing quality	☆	☆	☆	☆	☆
Overall	☆	☆	☆	☆	☆

POSTED AT:

_____

_____

_____

BOOK TITLE

Author

Genre

Date started   Date finished

REVIEW

_____

_____

_____

_____

_____

RATING

Plot	☆	☆	☆	☆	☆
Characters	☆	☆	☆	☆	☆
Originality	☆	☆	☆	☆	☆
Writing quality	☆	☆	☆	☆	☆
Overall	☆	☆	☆	☆	☆

POSTED AT :

_____

_____

_____

BOOK TITLE

Author

Genre

Date started   Date finished

REVIEW

_____

_____

_____

_____

_____

RATING

Plot   ☆ ☆ ☆ ☆ ☆
Characters   ☆ ☆ ☆ ☆ ☆
Originality   ☆ ☆ ☆ ☆ ☆
Writing quality ☆ ☆ ☆ ☆ ☆
Overall   ☆ ☆ ☆ ☆ ☆

POSTED AT :

_____

_____

_____

BOOK TITLE

Author

Genre

Date started   Date finished

REVIEW

_____

_____

_____

_____

_____

RATING

Plot   ☆ ☆ ☆ ☆ ☆
Characters   ☆ ☆ ☆ ☆ ☆
Originality   ☆ ☆ ☆ ☆ ☆
Writing quality ☆ ☆ ☆ ☆ ☆
Overall   ☆ ☆ ☆ ☆ ☆

POSTED AT :

_____

_____

_____

BOOK TITLE

Author

Genre

Date started   Date finished

REVIEW

_____

_____

_____

_____

_____

RATING

Plot   ☆ ☆ ☆ ☆ ☆
Characters   ☆ ☆ ☆ ☆ ☆
Originality   ☆ ☆ ☆ ☆ ☆
Writing quality ☆ ☆ ☆ ☆ ☆
Overall   ☆ ☆ ☆ ☆ ☆

POSTED AT:

_____

_____

_____

BOOK TITLE

Author

Genre

Date started   Date finished

REVIEW

_____

_____

_____

_____

_____

RATING

Plot   ☆ ☆ ☆ ☆ ☆
Characters   ☆ ☆ ☆ ☆ ☆
Originality   ☆ ☆ ☆ ☆ ☆
Writing quality ☆ ☆ ☆ ☆ ☆
Overall   ☆ ☆ ☆ ☆ ☆

POSTED AT :

_____

_____

_____

BOOK TITLE

Author

Genre

Date started   Date finished

REVIEW

_____

_____

_____

_____

_____

RATING

Plot	☆	☆	☆	☆	☆
Characters	☆	☆	☆	☆	☆
Originality	☆	☆	☆	☆	☆
Writing quality	☆	☆	☆	☆	☆
Overall	☆	☆	☆	☆	☆

POSTED AT :

_____

_____

_____

BOOK TITLE

Author

Genre

Date started   Date finished

REVIEW

RATING

Plot	☆ ☆ ☆ ☆ ☆
Characters	☆ ☆ ☆ ☆ ☆
Originality	☆ ☆ ☆ ☆ ☆
Writing quality	☆ ☆ ☆ ☆ ☆
Overall	☆ ☆ ☆ ☆ ☆

POSTED AT:

BOOK TITLE

Author _____

Genre _____

Date started _____ Date finished _____

REVIEW

_____

_____

_____

_____

_____

RATING

Plot	☆	☆	☆	☆	☆
Characters	☆	☆	☆	☆	☆
Originality	☆	☆	☆	☆	☆
Writing quality	☆	☆	☆	☆	☆
Overall	☆	☆	☆	☆	☆

POSTED AT :

_____

_____

_____

BOOK TITLE

Author

Genre

Date started   Date finished

REVIEW

_____

_____

_____

_____

_____

RATING

Plot   ☆ ☆ ☆ ☆ ☆
Characters   ☆ ☆ ☆ ☆ ☆
Originality   ☆ ☆ ☆ ☆ ☆
Writing quality ☆ ☆ ☆ ☆ ☆
Overall   ☆ ☆ ☆ ☆ ☆

POSTED AT:

_____

_____

_____

BOOK TITLE

Author

Genre

Date started   Date finished

REVIEW

RATING

Plot	☆	☆	☆	☆	☆
Characters	☆	☆	☆	☆	☆
Originality	☆	☆	☆	☆	☆
Writing quality	☆	☆	☆	☆	☆
Overall	☆	☆	☆	☆	☆

POSTED AT:

BOOK TITLE

Author

Genre

Date started   Date finished

REVIEW

_____

_____

_____

_____

_____

RATING

Plot   ☆ ☆ ☆ ☆ ☆
Characters   ☆ ☆ ☆ ☆ ☆
Originality   ☆ ☆ ☆ ☆ ☆
Writing quality   ☆ ☆ ☆ ☆ ☆
Overall   ☆ ☆ ☆ ☆ ☆

POSTED AT :

_____

_____

_____

BOOK TITLE

Author

Genre

Date started   Date finished

REVIEW

_____

_____

_____

_____

_____

RATING

Plot   ☆ ☆ ☆ ☆ ☆
Characters   ☆ ☆ ☆ ☆ ☆
Originality   ☆ ☆ ☆ ☆ ☆
Writing quality ☆ ☆ ☆ ☆ ☆
Overall   ☆ ☆ ☆ ☆ ☆

POSTED AT:

_____

_____

_____

BOOK TITLE

Author

Genre

Date started   Date finished

REVIEW

RATING

Plot	☆	☆	☆	☆	☆
Characters	☆	☆	☆	☆	☆
Originality	☆	☆	☆	☆	☆
Writing quality	☆	☆	☆	☆	☆
Overall	☆	☆	☆	☆	☆

POSTED AT:

BOOK TITLE

Author

Genre

Date started   Date finished

REVIEW

_____

_____

_____

_____

_____

RATING

Plot   ☆ ☆ ☆ ☆ ☆
Characters   ☆ ☆ ☆ ☆ ☆
Originality   ☆ ☆ ☆ ☆ ☆
Writing quality ☆ ☆ ☆ ☆ ☆
Overall   ☆ ☆ ☆ ☆ ☆

POSTED AT:

_____

_____

_____

BOOK TITLE

Author

Genre

Date started   Date finished

REVIEW

_____

_____

_____

_____

_____

RATING

Plot   ☆ ☆ ☆ ☆ ☆
Characters   ☆ ☆ ☆ ☆ ☆
Originality   ☆ ☆ ☆ ☆ ☆
Writing quality ☆ ☆ ☆ ☆ ☆
Overall   ☆ ☆ ☆ ☆ ☆

POSTED AT:

_____

_____

_____

BOOK TITLE

Author

Genre

Date started   Date finished

REVIEW

_____

_____

_____

_____

_____

RATING

Plot   ☆ ☆ ☆ ☆ ☆
Characters   ☆ ☆ ☆ ☆ ☆
Originality   ☆ ☆ ☆ ☆ ☆
Writing quality   ☆ ☆ ☆ ☆ ☆
Overall   ☆ ☆ ☆ ☆ ☆

POSTED AT:

_____

_____

_____

BOOK TITLE

Author

Genre

Date started   Date finished

REVIEW

RATING

Plot	☆ ☆ ☆ ☆ ☆
Characters	☆ ☆ ☆ ☆ ☆
Originality	☆ ☆ ☆ ☆ ☆
Writing quality	☆ ☆ ☆ ☆ ☆
Overall	☆ ☆ ☆ ☆ ☆

POSTED AT :

BOOK TITLE

Author

Genre

Date started   Date finished

REVIEW

_____

_____

_____

_____

_____

RATING

Plot   ☆ ☆ ☆ ☆ ☆
Characters   ☆ ☆ ☆ ☆ ☆
Originality   ☆ ☆ ☆ ☆ ☆
Writing quality ☆ ☆ ☆ ☆ ☆
Overall   ☆ ☆ ☆ ☆ ☆

POSTED AT :

_____

_____

_____

BOOK TITLE

Author

Genre

Date started   Date finished

REVIEW

_____

_____

_____

_____

_____

RATING

Plot	☆ ☆ ☆ ☆ ☆
Characters	☆ ☆ ☆ ☆ ☆
Originality	☆ ☆ ☆ ☆ ☆
Writing quality	☆ ☆ ☆ ☆ ☆
Overall	☆ ☆ ☆ ☆ ☆

POSTED AT :

_____

_____

_____

BOOK TITLE

Author

Genre

Date started   Date finished

REVIEW

_____

_____

_____

_____

_____

RATING

Plot   ☆ ☆ ☆ ☆ ☆
Characters   ☆ ☆ ☆ ☆ ☆
Originality   ☆ ☆ ☆ ☆ ☆
Writing quality ☆ ☆ ☆ ☆ ☆
Overall   ☆ ☆ ☆ ☆ ☆

POSTED AT :

_____

_____

_____

BOOK TITLE

Author

Genre

Date started   Date finished

REVIEW

_____

_____

_____

_____

_____

RATING

Plot   ☆ ☆ ☆ ☆ ☆
Characters   ☆ ☆ ☆ ☆ ☆
Originality   ☆ ☆ ☆ ☆ ☆
Writing quality ☆ ☆ ☆ ☆ ☆
Overall   ☆ ☆ ☆ ☆ ☆

POSTED AT :

_____

_____

_____

BOOK TITLE

Author

Genre

Date started   Date finished

REVIEW

_____

_____

_____

_____

_____

RATING

Plot   ☆ ☆ ☆ ☆ ☆
Characters   ☆ ☆ ☆ ☆ ☆
Originality   ☆ ☆ ☆ ☆ ☆
Writing quality ☆ ☆ ☆ ☆ ☆
Overall   ☆ ☆ ☆ ☆ ☆

POSTED AT :

_____

_____

_____

BOOK TITLE

Author

Genre

Date started   Date finished

REVIEW

_____

_____

_____

_____

_____

RATING

Plot   ☆ ☆ ☆ ☆ ☆
Characters   ☆ ☆ ☆ ☆ ☆
Originality   ☆ ☆ ☆ ☆ ☆
Writing quality   ☆ ☆ ☆ ☆ ☆
Overall   ☆ ☆ ☆ ☆ ☆

POSTED AT:

_____

_____

_____

BOOK TITLE

Author

Genre

Date started   Date finished

REVIEW

RATING

Plot	☆	☆	☆	☆	☆
Characters	☆	☆	☆	☆	☆
Originality	☆	☆	☆	☆	☆
Writing quality	☆	☆	☆	☆	☆
Overall	☆	☆	☆	☆	☆

POSTED AT :

BOOK TITLE

Author

Genre

Date started   Date finished

REVIEW

_____

_____

_____

_____

_____

RATING

Plot   ☆ ☆ ☆ ☆ ☆
Characters   ☆ ☆ ☆ ☆ ☆
Originality   ☆ ☆ ☆ ☆ ☆
Writing quality ☆ ☆ ☆ ☆ ☆
Overall   ☆ ☆ ☆ ☆ ☆

POSTED AT :

_____

_____

_____

BOOK TITLE

Author

Genre

Date started   Date finished

REVIEW

RATING

Plot   ☆ ☆ ☆ ☆ ☆
Characters   ☆ ☆ ☆ ☆ ☆
Originality   ☆ ☆ ☆ ☆ ☆
Writing quality ☆ ☆ ☆ ☆ ☆
Overall   ☆ ☆ ☆ ☆ ☆

POSTED AT:

BOOK TITLE

Author

Genre

Date started   Date finished

REVIEW

RATING

Plot   ☆ ☆ ☆ ☆ ☆
Characters   ☆ ☆ ☆ ☆ ☆
Originality   ☆ ☆ ☆ ☆ ☆
Writing quality ☆ ☆ ☆ ☆ ☆
Overall   ☆ ☆ ☆ ☆ ☆

POSTED AT:

BOOK TITLE

Author

Genre

Date started   Date finished

REVIEW

_____

_____

_____

_____

_____

RATING

Plot   ☆ ☆ ☆ ☆ ☆
Characters   ☆ ☆ ☆ ☆ ☆
Originality   ☆ ☆ ☆ ☆ ☆
Writing quality ☆ ☆ ☆ ☆ ☆
Overall   ☆ ☆ ☆ ☆ ☆

POSTED AT:

_____

_____

_____

BOOK TITLE

Author _____

Genre _____

Date started _____ Date finished _____

REVIEW

_____

_____

_____

_____

_____

RATING

Plot	☆	☆	☆	☆	☆
Characters	☆	☆	☆	☆	☆
Originality	☆	☆	☆	☆	☆
Writing quality	☆	☆	☆	☆	☆
Overall	☆	☆	☆	☆	☆

POSTED AT :

_____

_____

_____

BOOK TITLE

Author

Genre

Date started   Date finished

REVIEW

_____

_____

_____

_____

_____

RATING

Plot   ☆ ☆ ☆ ☆ ☆
Characters   ☆ ☆ ☆ ☆ ☆
Originality   ☆ ☆ ☆ ☆ ☆
Writing quality ☆ ☆ ☆ ☆ ☆
Overall   ☆ ☆ ☆ ☆ ☆

POSTED AT :

_____

_____

_____

BOOK TITLE

Author

Genre

Date started   Date finished

REVIEW

_____

_____

_____

_____

_____

RATING

Plot	☆	☆	☆	☆	☆
Characters	☆	☆	☆	☆	☆
Originality	☆	☆	☆	☆	☆
Writing quality	☆	☆	☆	☆	☆
Overall	☆	☆	☆	☆	☆

POSTED AT :

_____

_____

_____

BOOK TITLE

Author

Genre

Date started   Date finished

REVIEW

RATING

Plot   ☆ ☆ ☆ ☆ ☆
Characters   ☆ ☆ ☆ ☆ ☆
Originality   ☆ ☆ ☆ ☆ ☆
Writing quality ☆ ☆ ☆ ☆ ☆
Overall   ☆ ☆ ☆ ☆ ☆

POSTED AT :

BOOK TITLE

Author

Genre

Date started   Date finished

REVIEW

_____

_____

_____

_____

_____

RATING

Plot	☆ ☆ ☆ ☆ ☆
Characters	☆ ☆ ☆ ☆ ☆
Originality	☆ ☆ ☆ ☆ ☆
Writing quality	☆ ☆ ☆ ☆ ☆
Overall	☆ ☆ ☆ ☆ ☆

POSTED AT:

_____

_____

_____

BOOK TITLE

Author

Genre

Date started   Date finished

REVIEW

_____

_____

_____

_____

_____

RATING

Plot   ☆ ☆ ☆ ☆ ☆
Characters   ☆ ☆ ☆ ☆ ☆
Originality   ☆ ☆ ☆ ☆ ☆
Writing quality   ☆ ☆ ☆ ☆ ☆
Overall   ☆ ☆ ☆ ☆ ☆

POSTED AT:

_____

_____

_____

BOOK TITLE

Author

Genre

Date started   Date finished

REVIEW

RATING

Plot   ☆ ☆ ☆ ☆ ☆
Characters   ☆ ☆ ☆ ☆ ☆
Originality   ☆ ☆ ☆ ☆ ☆
Writing quality ☆ ☆ ☆ ☆ ☆
Overall   ☆ ☆ ☆ ☆ ☆

POSTED AT:

BOOK TITLE

Author

Genre

Date started   Date finished

REVIEW

RATING

Plot   ☆ ☆ ☆ ☆ ☆
Characters   ☆ ☆ ☆ ☆ ☆
Originality   ☆ ☆ ☆ ☆ ☆
Writing quality   ☆ ☆ ☆ ☆ ☆
Overall   ☆ ☆ ☆ ☆ ☆

POSTED AT :

BOOK TITLE

Author

Genre

Date started   Date finished

REVIEW

RATING

Plot   ☆ ☆ ☆ ☆ ☆
Characters   ☆ ☆ ☆ ☆ ☆
Originality   ☆ ☆ ☆ ☆ ☆
Writing quality ☆ ☆ ☆ ☆ ☆
Overall   ☆ ☆ ☆ ☆ ☆

POSTED AT :

BOOK TITLE

Author

Genre

Date started   Date finished

REVIEW

_____

_____

_____

_____

_____

RATING

Plot	☆	☆	☆	☆	☆
Characters	☆	☆	☆	☆	☆
Originality	☆	☆	☆	☆	☆
Writing quality	☆	☆	☆	☆	☆
Overall	☆	☆	☆	☆	☆

POSTED AT:

_____

_____

_____

BOOK TITLE

Author

Genre

Date started   Date finished

REVIEW

_____

_____

_____

_____

_____

RATING

Plot   ☆ ☆ ☆ ☆ ☆
Characters   ☆ ☆ ☆ ☆ ☆
Originality   ☆ ☆ ☆ ☆ ☆
Writing quality   ☆ ☆ ☆ ☆ ☆
Overall   ☆ ☆ ☆ ☆ ☆

POSTED AT:

_____

_____

_____

BOOK TITLE

Author

Genre

Date started   Date finished

REVIEW

_____

_____

_____

_____

_____

RATING

Plot	☆	☆	☆	☆	☆
Characters	☆	☆	☆	☆	☆
Originality	☆	☆	☆	☆	☆
Writing quality	☆	☆	☆	☆	☆
Overall	☆	☆	☆	☆	☆

POSTED AT:

_____

_____

_____

BOOK TITLE

Author

Genre

Date started   Date finished

REVIEW

_____

_____

_____

_____

_____

RATING

Plot   ☆ ☆ ☆ ☆ ☆
Characters   ☆ ☆ ☆ ☆ ☆
Originality   ☆ ☆ ☆ ☆ ☆
Writing quality   ☆ ☆ ☆ ☆ ☆
Overall   ☆ ☆ ☆ ☆ ☆

POSTED AT :

_____

_____

_____

BOOK TITLE

Author

Genre

Date started   Date finished

REVIEW

RATING

Plot	☆ ☆ ☆ ☆ ☆
Characters	☆ ☆ ☆ ☆ ☆
Originality	☆ ☆ ☆ ☆ ☆
Writing quality	☆ ☆ ☆ ☆ ☆
Overall	☆ ☆ ☆ ☆ ☆

POSTED AT:

BOOK TITLE

Author

Genre

Date started   Date finished

REVIEW

_____

_____

_____

_____

_____

RATING

Plot   ☆ ☆ ☆ ☆ ☆
Characters   ☆ ☆ ☆ ☆ ☆
Originality   ☆ ☆ ☆ ☆ ☆
Writing quality ☆ ☆ ☆ ☆ ☆
Overall   ☆ ☆ ☆ ☆ ☆

POSTED AT :

_____

_____

_____

BOOK TITLE

Author

Genre

Date started   Date finished

REVIEW

_____

_____

_____

_____

_____

RATING

Plot   ☆ ☆ ☆ ☆ ☆
Characters   ☆ ☆ ☆ ☆ ☆
Originality   ☆ ☆ ☆ ☆ ☆
Writing quality ☆ ☆ ☆ ☆ ☆
Overall   ☆ ☆ ☆ ☆ ☆

POSTED AT :

_____

_____

_____

BOOK TITLE

Author

Genre

Date started   Date finished

REVIEW

_____

_____

_____

_____

_____

RATING

Plot	☆	☆	☆	☆	☆
Characters	☆	☆	☆	☆	☆
Originality	☆	☆	☆	☆	☆
Writing quality	☆	☆	☆	☆	☆
Overall	☆	☆	☆	☆	☆

POSTED AT:

_____

_____

_____

BOOK TITLE

Author

Genre

Date started   Date finished

REVIEW

_____

_____

_____

_____

_____

RATING

Plot   ☆ ☆ ☆ ☆ ☆
Characters   ☆ ☆ ☆ ☆ ☆
Originality   ☆ ☆ ☆ ☆ ☆
Writing quality ☆ ☆ ☆ ☆ ☆
Overall   ☆ ☆ ☆ ☆ ☆

POSTED AT:

_____

_____

_____

BOOK TITLE

Author

Genre

Date started   Date finished

REVIEW

RATING

Plot	☆	☆	☆	☆	☆
Characters	☆	☆	☆	☆	☆
Originality	☆	☆	☆	☆	☆
Writing quality	☆	☆	☆	☆	☆
Overall	☆	☆	☆	☆	☆

POSTED AT :

BOOK TITLE

Author

Genre

Date started   Date finished

REVIEW

_____

_____

_____

_____

_____

RATING

Plot	☆	☆	☆	☆	☆
Characters	☆	☆	☆	☆	☆
Originality	☆	☆	☆	☆	☆
Writing quality	☆	☆	☆	☆	☆
Overall	☆	☆	☆	☆	☆

POSTED AT :

_____

_____

_____

BOOK TITLE

Author

Genre

Date started   Date finished

REVIEW

_____

_____

_____

_____

_____

RATING

Plot	☆	☆	☆	☆	☆
Characters	☆	☆	☆	☆	☆
Originality	☆	☆	☆	☆	☆
Writing quality	☆	☆	☆	☆	☆
Overall	☆	☆	☆	☆	☆

POSTED AT :

_____

_____

_____

BOOK TITLE

Author

Genre

Date started   Date finished

REVIEW

_____

_____

_____

_____

_____

RATING

Plot   ☆ ☆ ☆ ☆ ☆
Characters   ☆ ☆ ☆ ☆ ☆
Originality   ☆ ☆ ☆ ☆ ☆
Writing quality ☆ ☆ ☆ ☆ ☆
Overall   ☆ ☆ ☆ ☆ ☆

POSTED AT :

_____

_____

_____

BOOK TITLE

Author

Genre

Date started   Date finished

REVIEW

_____

_____

_____

_____

_____

RATING

Plot	☆	☆	☆	☆	☆
Characters	☆	☆	☆	☆	☆
Originality	☆	☆	☆	☆	☆
Writing quality	☆	☆	☆	☆	☆
Overall	☆	☆	☆	☆	☆

POSTED AT:

_____

_____

_____

BOOK TITLE

Author

Genre

Date started   Date finished

REVIEW

_____

_____

_____

_____

_____

RATING

Plot   ☆ ☆ ☆ ☆ ☆
Characters   ☆ ☆ ☆ ☆ ☆
Originality   ☆ ☆ ☆ ☆ ☆
Writing quality ☆ ☆ ☆ ☆ ☆
Overall   ☆ ☆ ☆ ☆ ☆

POSTED AT :

_____

_____

_____

BOOK TITLE

Author

Genre

Date started   Date finished

REVIEW

_____

_____

_____

_____

_____

RATING

Plot	☆	☆	☆	☆	☆
Characters	☆	☆	☆	☆	☆
Originality	☆	☆	☆	☆	☆
Writing quality	☆	☆	☆	☆	☆
Overall	☆	☆	☆	☆	☆

POSTED AT:

_____

_____

_____

BOOK TITLE

Author

Genre

Date started   Date finished

REVIEW

_____

_____

_____

_____

_____

RATING

Plot	☆ ☆ ☆ ☆ ☆
Characters	☆ ☆ ☆ ☆ ☆
Originality	☆ ☆ ☆ ☆ ☆
Writing quality	☆ ☆ ☆ ☆ ☆
Overall	☆ ☆ ☆ ☆ ☆

POSTED AT:

_____

_____

_____

BOOK TITLE

Author

Genre

Date started   Date finished

REVIEW

_____

_____

_____

_____

_____

RATING

Plot   ☆ ☆ ☆ ☆ ☆
Characters   ☆ ☆ ☆ ☆ ☆
Originality   ☆ ☆ ☆ ☆ ☆
Writing quality ☆ ☆ ☆ ☆ ☆
Overall   ☆ ☆ ☆ ☆ ☆

POSTED AT :

_____

_____

_____

BOOK TITLE

Author

Genre

Date started   Date finished

REVIEW

_____

_____

_____

_____

_____

RATING

Plot	☆	☆	☆	☆	☆
Characters	☆	☆	☆	☆	☆
Originality	☆	☆	☆	☆	☆
Writing quality	☆	☆	☆	☆	☆
Overall	☆	☆	☆	☆	☆

POSTED AT :

_____

_____

_____

BOOK TITLE

Author

Genre

Date started   Date finished

REVIEW

_____

_____

_____

_____

_____

RATING

Plot	☆	☆	☆	☆	☆
Characters	☆	☆	☆	☆	☆
Originality	☆	☆	☆	☆	☆
Writing quality	☆	☆	☆	☆	☆
Overall	☆	☆	☆	☆	☆

POSTED AT:

_____

_____

_____

BOOK TITLE

Author

Genre

Date started   Date finished

REVIEW

_____

_____

_____

_____

_____

RATING

Plot   ☆ ☆ ☆ ☆ ☆
Characters   ☆ ☆ ☆ ☆ ☆
Originality   ☆ ☆ ☆ ☆ ☆
Writing quality ☆ ☆ ☆ ☆ ☆
Overall   ☆ ☆ ☆ ☆ ☆

POSTED AT :

_____

_____

_____

BOOK TITLE

Author

Genre

Date started   Date finished

REVIEW

RATING

Plot	☆ ☆ ☆ ☆ ☆
Characters	☆ ☆ ☆ ☆ ☆
Originality	☆ ☆ ☆ ☆ ☆
Writing quality	☆ ☆ ☆ ☆ ☆
Overall	☆ ☆ ☆ ☆ ☆

POSTED AT :

BOOK TITLE

Author

Genre

Date started   Date finished

REVIEW

_____

_____

_____

_____

_____

RATING

Plot   ☆ ☆ ☆ ☆ ☆
Characters   ☆ ☆ ☆ ☆ ☆
Originality   ☆ ☆ ☆ ☆ ☆
Writing quality ☆ ☆ ☆ ☆ ☆
Overall   ☆ ☆ ☆ ☆ ☆

POSTED AT:

_____

_____

_____

BOOK TITLE

Author

Genre

Date started   Date finished

REVIEW

_____

_____

_____

_____

_____

RATING

Plot	☆	☆	☆	☆	☆
Characters	☆	☆	☆	☆	☆
Originality	☆	☆	☆	☆	☆
Writing quality	☆	☆	☆	☆	☆
Overall	☆	☆	☆	☆	☆

POSTED AT :

_____

_____

_____

Wait for the Lord; be strong and take heart, and wait for the Lord.

PSALM 27 : 14

2021
YEAR IN REVIEW

A Peek in the Mirror

FAVORITE BOOKS

_____
_____
_____
_____
_____

FAVORITE QUOTE

_____
_____
_____
_____
_____
_____
_____
_____
_____
_____

FAVORITE NEW AUTHORS

BEST NEW RELEASES

GREATEST SURPRISE

Books Upon Books

TOTAL BOOKS READ

GENRE	# OF BOOKS
_____	_____
_____	_____
_____	_____
_____	_____
_____	_____
_____	_____

TOTAL BOOKS REVIEWED

AVERAGE RATING ☆ ☆ ☆ ☆ ☆

ENJOYABLE LAUNCH TEAMS

_____

_____

_____

_____

_____

_____

_____

_____

For I am convinced that neither death nor life, neither angels nor demons, neither the present nor the future, nor any powers, neither height nor depth, nor anything else in all creation, will be able to separate us from the love of God that is in Christ Jesus our Lord.

ROMANS 8 : 38-39

THE BEST

OF THE BEST

Literary Face-Off

☆ ☆ ☆ ☆ ☆

☆ ☆ ☆ ☆ ☆

☆ ☆ ☆ ☆ ☆

☆ ☆ ☆ ☆ ☆

☆ ☆ ☆ ☆ ☆

☆ ☆ ☆ ☆ ☆

☆ ☆ ☆ ☆ ☆

☆ ☆ ☆ ☆ ☆

☆ ☆ ☆ ☆ ☆

Follow the path to your favorite book of the year by filling in each box with a book you enjoyed and deciding which books advance to the next round.

☆ ☆ ☆ ☆ ☆

☆ ☆ ☆ ☆ ☆

☆ ☆ ☆ ☆ ☆

Literary Face-Off

☆ ☆ ☆ ☆ ☆

☆ ☆ ☆ ☆ ☆

☆ ☆ ☆ ☆ ☆

AND THE WINNER IS:

THIS YEAR'S GREAT BOOKS

☆ ☆ ☆ ☆ ☆

☆ ☆ ☆ ☆ ☆

☆ ☆ ☆ ☆ ☆

title

author

Favorite Quotes

_____

_____

_____

_____

_____

_____

_____

_____

_____

_____

_____

_____

_____

_____

_____

_____

_____

_____

_____

_____

_____

_____

_____

_____

Favorite Quotes

Favorite Quotes

Favorite Quotes

_____

_____

_____

_____

_____

_____

_____

_____

_____

_____

_____

_____

_____

_____

_____

_____

_____

_____

_____

_____

Favorite Quotes

_____
_____
_____
_____
_____
_____
_____
_____
_____
_____
_____
_____
_____
_____
_____
_____
_____
_____
_____
_____
_____
_____

Favorite Quotes

_____

_____

_____

_____

_____

_____

_____

_____

_____

_____

_____

_____

_____

_____

_____

_____

_____

_____

Favorite Quotes

Favorite Quotes

_____

_____

_____

_____

_____

_____

_____

_____

_____

_____

_____

_____

_____

_____

_____

_____

_____

_____

Favorite Quotes

Favorite Quotes

_____

_____

_____

_____

_____

_____

_____

_____

_____

_____

_____

_____

_____

_____

_____

_____

_____

_____

"For I know the plans I have for you," declares the Lord, "plans to prosper you and not to harm you, plans to give you hope and a future."

JEREMIAH 29 : 11

2022

THE COMING YEAR

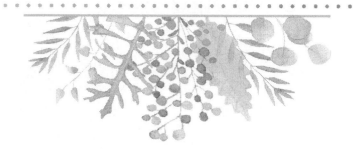

A Glance Ahead

HIGHLY ANTICIPATED NEW RELEASES

_____

_____

_____

_____

_____

UPCOMING EVENTS

_____

_____

_____

ONE NEW AUTHOR TO TRY

_____

Book Wishlist

GENRE

-
-
-
-
-
-
-
-
-
-
-
-
-
-

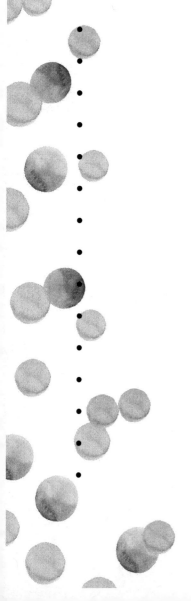

Book Wishlist

GENRE

-
-
-
-
-
-
-
-
-
-
-
-

Book Wishlist

GENRE

-
-
-
-
-
-
-
-
-
-
-
-
-
-

For we know that if our earthly house
of this tabernacle were dissolved,
we have a building of God,
a house not made with hands,
eternal in the heavens.

2 CORINTHIANS 5 : 1

MOSAIC

JOIN THE FAMILY

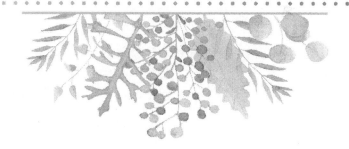

JOHNNIE ALEXANDER
www.johnnie-alexander.com

BRENDA S. ANDERSON
www.brendaandersonbooks.com

ELEANOR BERTIN
www.eleanorbertinauthor.com

SARA DAVISON
www.saradavison.org

JANICE L DICK
www.janicedick.com

DEB ELKINK
www.debelkink.com

CHAUTONA HAVIG
www.chautona.com

REGINA RUDD MERRICK
www.reginaruddmerrick.com

ANGELA D. MEYER
www.angeladmeyer.com

STACY MONSON
www.stacymonson.com

LORNA SEILSTAD
www.lornaseilstad.com

MARION UECKERMANN
www.marionueckermann.net

CANDACE WEST
www.candaceweststoryteller.com

KEEP IN TOUCH

Subscribe to *Grace & Glory* to receive updates about Mosaic's newest releases, events, and giveaways.
www.mosaiccollectionbooks.com/grace-glory

Join the Mosaic reader community on Facebook.
www.facebook.com/groups/themosaiccollection

To learn more about each author and to discover her books, visit
www.mosaiccollectionbooks.com/about-the-authors

WE'D LOVE TO HEAR FROM YOU

We'd appreciate your feedback as we design Mosaic's 2022 companion journal. We invite your comments at
www.mosaiccollectionbooks.com/totally-booked

Notes

Notes

Notes

Notes

Notes

Notes

Manufactured by Amazon.ca
Bolton, ON

16072528R00192